Bloodlines

The Sapphire Heirloom

A NOVEL BY

Zebulun McNeill

Bloodlines - The Sapphire Heirloom is a work of fiction. Names, characters, places, and incidents either are products of the author's imagination or are used fictitiously. Any resemblance to actual persons, living or dead, events, or locales is entirely coincidental.

ISBN: 979-8-218-27267-8

First Edition, Hardcover Print

To my sister, Avery, who has been my best friend and confidante for many tumultuous years. I'm glad our parents decided to keep you when you were born.

To my nephew, Sterling, who's currently too young to read, much less comprehend what writing even is to begin with. You're a pretty cool kid. I love you, buddy.

To my sister's wife, Cassie, for hyping me up and supporting me through the whole process of writing this damn thing, and offering to proofread and edit.

To my parents, for giving me just the right mix of mental illnesses through their genetic material, allowing me to write this book in the span of less than a week. I couldn't have done it without y'all.

To everybody else I may have forgotten, everybody I've met and engaged with over the years. Honestly? Most of you fucking suck. Some of y'all are cool, though.

I love you.

Prologue

Hundreds of years before the renowned artistry and enlightenment of Renaissance Italy, in the parched outskirts of a timeless desert, a story was sculpted, one nearly swallowed whole by the relentless march of time and the ever-shifting sands. This was not just any desert but a vast expanse where legends were born and died, and where the line between the tangible and the ethereal seemed to dance like a mirage upon the horizon.

In the heart of this desert, nestled amongst the sun-kissed dunes, stood a city of sandstone and mystery. Here, stories of a man named Valerius echoed through its labyrinthine alleys. A man whose very name would send shivers down the spines of the bravest souls, he was the embodiment of ambition, a man whose dreams soared higher than the desert hawks. His gaze, it was said, was deep and penetrating, revealing ambitions that transcended the realm of mere earthly desires.

In his quest for the epitome of power and splendor, Valerius sought the brilliance of the city's most distinguished gemologist. He painted visions of unimaginable affluence, compelling the craftsman with the allure of gold and the unspoken threats lurking in the shadows of his intense gaze. For days and nights, the gemologist, both awed and frightened, toiled. His efforts bore fruit in the form of a sapphire pendant of mesmerizing beauty, its cerulean core seemingly holding the enigmas of the cosmos itself.

Yet, for Valerius, the pendant's physical beauty was but a fraction of its intended grandeur. His dream transcended aesthetics; he envisioned a talisman of boundless might. To realize this vision, he turned to the city's enigmatic figure, Malachi – a man said to be more enigma than flesh, whose aura was steeped in forbidden lore. Under a starless sky, through chants older than the city itself, Malachi summoned the arcane to endow the sapphire with powers from the abyss. As the ritual reached its zenith, Valerius expressed his ultimate desire: to intertwine his very soul with the gem, ensuring that his reign of terror would defy even death's embrace.

Decades passed. With the pendant nestled against his chest, Valerius experienced the intoxicating duality of omnipotence and dread. Yet, time, the ultimate leveller, claimed him as it does all. With his passing, the infernal bond was eternally solidified. The pendant, with Valerius's tormented soul ensnared within its crystalline prison, lay in wait for its next chapter, its next wielder.

As empires rose and fell, as sands shifted and covered the relics of yore, the pendant lay buried, its sinister heartbeat a faint whisper, yearning for the day it would rise and cast its shadow once more.

Chapter 1

In the heart of Venice, where secrets danced with shadows, the Morosini family stood on the cusp of a fate they could neither foresee nor escape. The labyrinthine canals mirrored their lives - intertwined, unpredictable, and flowing inexorably towards a future where every choice would carry weight and consequence. Yet, as the golden hues of the late afternoon sun gilded the city's spires, all seemed tranquil, and the looming tide of destiny remained unnoticed by most.

The Morosini's palazzo stood proudly at the edge of one of the many canals winding through the city. A tall, ornate structure of stone, glistening in the brilliant summer sun and reflecting against the water. The palazzo has been in the Morosini family for several generations, having been built from the ground up from the first of the family that made the pilgrimage to Venice.

Elegant archways carved into the building's facade, decorated with plentiful crosses and carved images of ivy crawling around the pillars, many of which were nothing more than decoration. Despite the apparent opulence, the Morosini palazzo was only one of many similar buildings, owned by many other families. Even though the family held significant status against the regular humdrum of the city streets, they were still just another group of faces when compared to the rest of the Venetian elites - a fact that the matriarch of the family is all too familiar with.

The interior of the palazzo continues to unfurl in a wondrous showcase of the Morosini status. A spectacular display of Venetian tiling, kept to a near polish by the many servants quietly sprinting through the vast and empty halls, gave way to room after room of decor and splendour.

From a grand chandelier that hung with an elegance demanding attention, to intricately carved wooden panels depicting family heraldry, the grandeur of the Morosini lineage was evident in every nook and corner. It was here, in the embrace of such affluence, that the members of the Morosini household lived and loved, each unique, yet bound together by the weight of their name.

Leonora Morosini stood as the formidable pillar of the Morosini legacy. In the palatial drawing room, her silhouette, often backlit by the warm glow of candles, was an embodiment of authority. Every piece of jewellery, every fold of her richly embroidered gown seemed to accentuate her stature, both in the family and in Venetian society. Yet, her eyes, those astute gatekeepers of a thousand secrets, revealed a hint of vulnerability that only a few ever witnessed.

Just a few chambers away, where the fragrant aroma of oils and canvases intertwined, Giovanni Morosini found his sanctuary. He, with his tousled chestnut hair and a gaze often lost in thought, was the family's artist and dreamer. Amidst his brushes and paints, he sought and found solace, even as he grappled with the dual life of an heir and a lover in secret.

In contrast, the laughter and light footsteps that often echoed from the palazzo's balcony belonged to Liliana

Morosini. Resplendent in her beauty and spirit, she was a dazzling blend of Morosini pride and youthful rebellion. Her nights spent gazing at the moonlit canals, she dreamt of horizons beyond the Venetian lagoons, her heart ever curious about a world she knew far too little about.

As the day slowly yawns into an early twilight, the bright gates of the Morosini estate creaked open to admit a carriage. It bore no insignia, yet its somber elegance spoke of old money and lineage. From it descended a woman. She stood tall and statuesque, draped in black mourning garments that flowed around her like liquid shadows. Her face, though aged, retained the classic beauty of Venetian aristocracy.

But there was something distinctly enigmatic about her. While others would gleam in the soft golden hue of the setting sun, she seemed to evade its touch, her figure bathed in an almost ethereal coolness. Around her neck, a pendant - that of a gem, deep and purple. Curiosity at the unexpected arrival spread through the household.

From the vantage of the balcony, Leonora caught sight of the mysterious figure approaching the palazzo's entrance. Her demeanour always unyielding and vigilant, she descended the grand staircase with all the grace and authority of a queen, the soft rustling of her gown the only sound to fill the anticipatory silence. "Good evening, madam," Leonora began, addressing the woman with a measured politeness, keeping her guard up. "Our estate does not often receive visitors at such an hour, especially ones unknown to us. Might I inquire as to the nature of your visit?"

The mysterious woman offered a subtle smile, one that hinted at ancient secrets and stories untold. "Leonora Morosini," she began, emphasising each syllable, "you may not know of me, but our families' histories intertwined in ways you cannot fathom. I have come to return something that was never truly mine to keep."

Perturbed by the knowledge of her own name yet strongly intrigued, Leonora gestured for the woman to enter. "Very well. If your intentions are sincere, you are welcome in the house of Morosini."

Servants rushed forward, taking the woman's cloak and revealing her in full splendour beneath the grand chandelier. The opulence of the household seemed to echo and respond to her very presence, as though the walls themselves recognised a formidable player in the age-old game of power and prestige. The entire palazzo was abuzz, keen on learning more about the welcomed intruder.

"My name is Cecelia Adriana."

****

The most fleeting thought of orange peels and raspberry stems hung in the air, breathing ever so quietly from the bowl of potpourri on the cedar heartwood table that featured prominently in the centre of the room. Surrounded by this bowl were a handful of beautifully carved beeswax candles, alight with the softest of glows - providing just enough light to illuminate the immediate surroundings, but not so much that it became overbearing against the contrast of the darkening room.

Surrounding the table gathered the Morosini family and their guest, seated upon an assortment of chairs each constructed of polished mahogany and upholstered with a dark cherry coloured felt, stuffed with an exotic goose down, resulting in a seat upon which you could rest for a near eternity without the faintest realisation of having been seated for too long. In the far side of the room, a fireplace popped and crackled with the tales of a hundred years witnessed by the lumber from the trees that fed it, offering forward a beautiful orange glow to contrast the candlelight. The sound of heels on polished tile echoed quickly through the room as one of the many servants ushered a silver tray laden with several ornate glasses, each of which were filled with a deep burgundy wine.

As the glasses were placed delicately in front of each member of the gathering, Leonora eyed their mysterious guest, her thoughts racing as she attempted to glean every ounce of insight she could possibly extract from the folds of Cecelia's wizened facial features. At first glance she had the appearance of a typical old Venetian woman, though there seemed to be something not entirely right with her. Perhaps it was the way the shadows danced and twirled across her face, or the air of perfected stillness she seemed to carry about her.

Lifting the glass that was placed before her, Leonora began. "Cecelia, is it?" Her voice broke the silence, reverberating through the walls of the room with all of the authority that only a matriarch could muster. "What brings you to my family's estate at this time of day?" Even though the Morosini's held a high enough social status that visitors had a tendency to drop by on a semi-regular basis to their household, it was still fairly unusual for the family to have guests this late in the day - most people were usually attending to their own at this time, so there wasn't much in the way of unannounced guests at a late hour.

"Firstly, I'd like to thank you for inviting me in to your estate at such an inopportune time. I hope I'm not bothering you," Cecelia responded, as she lifted her own glass of wine before taking a sip, eyeing the Morosini family that had gathered with her, measuring each of them with a keen eye. "I've come to return something to you. Or rather, to relinquish it - it's high time that it's in the hands if it's rightful owners," Cecelia continued. As she did, she set down her glass and began to lift a silver chain from around her neck, at the end of which dangled a piece of cut sapphire roughly the size of a small child's fist, wrapped in an intricate silver wiring.

Having always had a keen taste for objects of a certain beauty, Leonora's attention was drawn from their guest and focused intently on the pendant. The purplish glow it appeared to give off due to the flickering candlelight was particularly captivating. Puzzled yet intrigued, Leonora asked "You wish to return… this?" Surely the strange woman would have some sort of reason for her unannounced appearance paired with an offer of jewellery.

"Yes," said Cecelia. "This heirloom has been in the hands of my family, and most recently my own hands, for several generations. But it's not something that belongs to me or mine, it should find its true home comfortably here with you, the Morosinis." As she said this, Cecelia extended the necklace to Leonora who reached out to take it tentatively. As Leonora grabbed the sapphire, the air seemed abuzz with an ever-so-slightly intangible hum for the briefest of moments, before subsiding back into its typical stillness.

"It truly is a beautiful necklace," said Leonora. "But why us, and why now of all times?" She was right. The hour was getting late, and the mysteriousness surrounding the unannounced arrival and the offering was a touch too conspicuous. Even still, Leonora's interest was certainly piqued as her fingers ran across the chain and danced over the wiring that surrounded the sapphire, its weight quite prominent in her delicate hands.

"I'm afraid that the details are far too numerous and complex for tonight," Cecelia said. "Essentially, this heirloom was once in your family many generations ago. At some point, it came to be held by my family, and remained as such for many years. After many years, it's provided so very much for me, yet also brought about far too much grief. I am the last remaining member of my family, and as such I feel that it's high time to return the heirloom to its rightful owners."

As Cecelia explained this, Leonora passed the heirloom over to each member of her family, each of which felt an equal attraction to it, before it cycled back over into Leonora's possession. "You say that it's brought you grief, but how can that be?"

"My darling Leonora, everything under the sun has a price. It doesn't matter what the price is, just that the price must be paid. While the heirloom has certainly elevated my own status, it wasn't without cost." Cecelia remained steadfast with her dramatic flair, much to the slight annoyance of Leonora, who internally dismissed her as just a mad widow.

"We're certainly no strangers to dealing with grief or struggle due to our wealth or status," Leonora offered, vaguely gesturing to the lone watchman standing guard by the main door of the chamber. "If what you say about this necklace being part of our family is true, then we graciously accept its return." At this, Cecelia offered a slow toothy grin, pleased to be relieved of her burden as the necklace found its new home with its rightful owner.

"Very well, it would seem that everything is finally in place. With that, I believe I should be on my way," said Cecelia. As she slowly rose from her chair, the Morosini family did the same, and they all escorted her back to her carriage. As Cecelia lifted herself back into her carriage, the sun had already set and the only light that could be seen was that of candlelight from the neighbouring buildings. As the horses drew the carriage away with Cecelia and the crunch of hooves and wheels on gravel could be heard echoing against the walls of the Morosini palazzo, the family turned their backs to the entrance of their estate and walked back to the main hall, each puzzled by the visitation.

****

A few days have passed since the mysterious arrival and departure of Cecelia Adriana, and while she is mostly nothing more than a memory, talk of her appearance is still heard through the halls every so often between some of the house's servants, usually at a volume that's nothing more than a hushed whisper. At the end of one of these halls, is found the office and studio space of Giovanni Morosini.

Against every wall is a bookshelf that reaches from floor to ceiling, with each shelf packed with various books, scrolls, tomes, and oddities that Giovanni's collected over the years. In one corner of the room is Giovanni's desk, a solid slab of heavy polished oak, carved and curved into a soft edge, strewn with stacks of ink-stained papers containing sketches and diagrams, many of which were done by Giovanni himself.

Giovanni has always had an interest in the obscure. As the intellectual of the family, he spends a good majority of his time piecing together sketches of various insects, or studying mathematical formulas, or rummaging through one of the city's many libraries in order to gain any ounce of newfound knowledge, so it comes as no surprise that his study is littered with a wide cluster of odds and ends.

As the dedicated scratching of a quill pen fills what's left of the empty space, Giovanni is found leaning intently over one of the few remaining blank sheets of parchment, busily scrawling out the latest of his sketches. Positioned carefully on a small stand in front of him lies the sapphire necklace. Enraptured by its beauty, Giovanni felt the urge to translate his emotions into paper and ink, capturing the mesmerising beauty of the necklace forever into the stillness of a page.

Pen plunges into ink, and is hurriedly and pointedly scrawled across the surface of the parchment, Giovanni's hand racing back and forth as the line-work is slowly brought to life, each intricate detail being given a fresh breath of life through the lens of Giovanni's creative vision, his eyes darting between the physical necklace and its drawn recreation. A movement too quick, and he sends the bottle of ink flying off the desk and halfway across the room, little black droplets scattering across the pages and leaving a trail of splatter in its wake.

"Shit," Giovanni exclaimed, diving over to the fallen bottle to prevent it from spilling more ink. The moment that the bottle is lifted and returned back to its place on the desk, Giovanni dashes over to collect a bucket of water and a rag in order to wash up as much of the ink as he can before it dries into the flooring. The previous sketches, though splattered, are still salvageable enough for his liking. "Shit," he mutters as he sloshes the water from the bucket and onto the floor, the rag dragging back and forth across the ink, mopping up small amounts of it at a time. "I really need to be more careful."

As Giovanni mops up the last of the spilled ink on the floor, he looks up at the sapphire on his desk, his heart beating from the unexpected exertion. As he does so, a small ray of light from a nearby window catches the edge of the sapphire, which reflects the sunlight back out, scattering it across the room in a beautifully deep blue hue. Giovanni's breath is caught at the beauty of the sight, the warm blue dancing and reflecting across his face as he stares deep into the heart of the sapphire. For the briefest of moments, it seems as though the interior of the sapphire shifts and moves, dancing a sweet waltz with the sunlight that hits it. Unnoticed by her brother, Liliana steps into the room. "Giovanni? What are you doing on the floor?"

Suddenly brought out of the trance, Giovanni was startled briefly. "Oh, Liliana! I didn't hear you walk in. I was busy sketching the sapphire, and accidentally knocked over some ink, so I had just finished cleaning up the mess," he laughed. The eldest Morosini sibling is usually far more careful and deliberate than this, but there was something about the allure of the sapphire that had caused him to both hold and lose his focus entirely.

Liliana walks briskly over to Giovanni, offering a hand to lift him to his feet. As she pulls him up, she glances over to the sapphire on his desk. "I was wondering where it ran off to," she said. "Why do you think that old lady gave it to us anyway?" Liliana glides over to the desk to pick up the sapphire, getting a better look at it. As she grabs the sapphire, there's a fleeting sensation - a whispered chill - that runs up the length of her arm and down her spine. A hinted wash of emotions flow through her - curiosity, longing, and perhaps a breath of fear. The gem's been floating heavily through her mind ever since it's arrival, so she's excited at having the opportunity to once again have it in her possession, inspecting it like an amateur gemologist.

"I'm not too sure," said Giovanni, "but it's certainly an interesting piece of jewellery." Giovanni strides over to his desk, picking up the scattered papers, readjusting them and stacking them in an effort to make his workspace a touch more organised than the state it found itself in after the ink bottle was sent flying across the room.

"There you are," says Leonora, startling the siblings. They hadn't heard her enter the room behind them. "I've been looking all over for the two of you. I saw that the necklace wasn't where I had left it, and had figured one of you were off playing with it." Leonora walks over to Liliana, relinquishing the gem from her grasp, and holding it up in the sunlight, again releasing the deep blue glow to scatter across the room.

"Sorry mother," said Giovanni. "I was intrigued by it, and wanted to use it to practice my drawing." Giovanni reaches for the unfinished sketch of the sapphire, and presents it to Leonora. "I got distracted and accidentally spilled some ink, but it's all been cleaned up."

"It's no matter," says Leonora dismissively. "Perhaps you can finish your drawing in the morning." With that, Leonora turns to leave the study, leaving the Morosini siblings behind. The sound of her footsteps echo through the halls of palazzo, as she approaches her bedroom. Sitting on her nightstand is a small ornate jewellery box, with two tiny glass doors on the front. Opening this, she places the sapphire back in its resting place, before turning to her nightly duties.

As the sapphire glows faintly in the gentlest of moonlight, the Morosini palazzo seems to vibrate with a nearly imperceptible hum. The sapphire heirloom has finally found its way back into the possession of its rightful heirs. Unbeknown to the family, changes have been set into motion that cannot be reversed, changes that will forever rewrite the tale of the Morosinis.

Chapter 2

Venice greeted the day with a burst of gold. The first rays of dawn painted the azure canals, bouncing off the water to strike the gothic facades of the city's palazzos. Boats of every imaginable kind started their ballet on the water, as merchants, fishermen, and noble gondoliers prepared for the day's trade.

Inside the Morosini estate, the household had just started to come alive. Maids bustled about with linen, and cooks were already hard at work, the aromas of fresh breads and brewing coffees filling the air. Footsteps echoed across marble floors, each member of the household rising to their respective duties.

It was Leonora who first caught sight of the messenger. She had been enjoying her morning ritual, sipping tea by the vast window overlooking the canal, when a boat unlike the usual market ferries approached. The vessel was ornate, dark wood polished to a shine, with a lantern at the helm bearing the distinct insignia of a silver bell.

As the boat drew nearer, the silhouette of its sole passenger became clearer: a young man, no older than twenty, dressed in the plum and gold of the Bellini family. His eyes darted nervously as he adjusted the scroll case secured under his arm.

Leonora set her tea aside, her heartbeat quickening just a touch. She knew the Bellini emblem well - a symbol of considerable wealth and influence in Venice. A visit from a member of the Bellini household, even if it were just a messenger, was significant.

By the time the young man moored his boat and stepped onto the Morosini estate, a small entourage had gathered to greet him, led by Leonora herself. The way he carried himself - with a careful balance of deference and pride - suggested he understood the weight of his task. "You bring tidings from the House of Bellini?" Leonora inquired, her voice betraying none of her curiosity.

The young man bowed, his face flush with the donor of addressing the Morosini matriarch directly. "I do, Signora Morosini," he replied, extending the scroll case. "A letter from Master Antonio Bellini himself."

She accepted the letter, her fingers brushing against the cool wax of the Bellini seal - a silver bell against a deep purple backdrop. The weight of the parchment hinted at the importance of its contents. Unsealing it with a practiced hand, Leonora took a moment to read through the ornate script. The words flowed elegantly, filled with flourishes befitting the Bellini reputation.

As she read, the atmosphere in the room grew palpable with anticipation. Servants exchanged glances, and even the stoic guards at the entrance leaned in subtly. Leonora's face remained impassive, revealing nothing, but when she finally looked up, her gaze was sharp, intent. "It appears we are to expect a visit from Antonio Bellini himself," she announced. "He wishes to discuss a matter of mutual interest."

The news sent a ripple of excitement through the household. Antonio Bellini's name was synonymous with wealth, power, and shrewd business acumen. Rumours of his merchant ventures reached far and wide, from the spice traders of the East to the textile markets of Flanders. A personal visit from such a figure was no small event.

However, with this honour also came a touch of apprehension. What could be so vital that it would compel the illustrious merchant to visit the Morosini family personally? Speculation began to mount. Whispers traveled like wildfire, and by noon, the entire estate was abuzz.

Leonora retreated to her private chambers, the letter's contents weighing on her mind. She knew the implications of this visit, and while the rest of the household might see opportunity, she saw the delicate dance of politics and power. The game was afoot, and the Morosini family and been drawn into its whirlwind.

With the day still young, preparations began in earnest. The prospect of Antonio Bellini's arrival set a new pace for the household, and as the Venetian sun reached its zenith, Leonora, ever the meticulous planner, summoned her trusted circle of aides. The vast drawing room, with its high vaulted ceilings and frescoes depicting Morosini achievements, became a war room of sorts.

"Antonio Bellini's visit is not a casual affair," she began, her voice commanding the room's attention. "We must ensure that every corner, every shadow of our residence showcases the legacy and stature of the Morosini name. And above all, we must highlight our heritage, the jewel of our lineage."

Her mind wandered to the sapphire heirloom, its deep blue depths catching the light in mesmerising patterns. It was currently housed in a modest display case within her private chambers. Its relocation would not just be a matter of pride, but a statement of the family's claim to nobility and respect.

Leonora turned to Giovanni, who had always possessed a keen eye for aesthetics. "I want the heirloom to be placed in the grand salon, atop the central pedestal. Ensure it is well-lit, casting its glow for all to see. It must be the centrepiece of our presentation." Giovanni nodded in understanding. Having previously sketched its myriad facets, he held a quiet reverence for the gem. This was yet another opportunity to present it in its full splendour.

Around the palazzo, a hive of activity began. Servants were instructed to polish every surface until it gleamed. The gardens were to be tended to, ensuring that every blossom and blade of grass stood at attention. Chefs were directed to prepare an exquisite menu, one that would tantalise the palate of the discerning, well-traveled merchant.

Liliana, ever eager to be involved, took it upon herself to oversee the arrangements of the guest chambers. She selected the finest linens and ensured fresh flowers adorned every table. The scent of jasmine and roses wafted through the corridors, creating an ambiance of opulence and serenity.

Yet amidst the whirlwind of preparations, Leonora remained a beacon of calm. She understood the nuances of Venetian society, where every gesture and display carried significant weight. Aligning with Antonio Bellini could propel the Morosini family into new realms of influence. This was not just a visit; it was a pivotal moment.

The day progressed, and as the shadows lengthened, Leonora took a moment to survey the transformed estate.

The sapphire, now occupying its pride of place in the grand salon, seemed to pulse with an inner light, a beacon drawing all eyes towards it. It was a symbol, not just of their wealth, but of the Morosini's long and storied past.

A sense of expectancy filled the air. The Morosini estate, having undergone its metamorphosis, now stood ready to receive its distinguished guest. Every light, every reflection, seemed to whisper of promises and potential alliances. The stage was set, and the Morosini family awaited the arrival of Antonio Bellini with bated breath.

****

Venice, in its golden age, was a city of dreams, powered largely by its merchants. The intricate network of canals that stitched the city together echoed with tales of distant lands, whispered by sailors and sung aloud by bards. Those who mastered the tides of commerce were the true kings and queens of this floating city, and among them, the Bellinis were legends.

To be a merchant in Venice was not merely about trade. It was an art, a dance of diplomacy and strategy. Each deal was a brushstroke on the canvas of the city's ever-evolving narrative. And for the Bellinis, this canvas was a masterpiece. They did not just sell silks and spices; they sold dreams, stories, and promises. They were architects of fate, building empires not just on the solid foundation of gold, but on the shifting sands of influence and connections.

Antonio Bellini was the latest in this illustrious line. From a young age, he was groomed to be more than just a merchant. He was a strategist, a visionary, always two steps ahead of his contemporaries. His reputation was that of a golden hawk - sharp-eyed, majestic, and ever watchful. To many, he was Venice's golden son, a beacon of ambition and success. Yet, beneath the sheen of prosperity, there existed a relentless drive, a hunger for more - more power, more influence, more legacy.

As the sun began its descent, casting long shadows over the Morosini estate, a procession appeared on the horizon. At its helm was a grand carriage, emblazoned with the insignia of the Bellini family. Following the carriage was an entourage of attendants, each dressed in finery that spoke of wealth and taste. The clattering of hooves and the murmuring of the crowd became a symphony announcing Antonio's arrival.

The Morosini family assembled at the entrance, anticipation evident in their postures. As the carriage came to a halt, the door opened to reveal Antonio. Dressed in a rich brocade jacket, his dark hair slicked back, he exuded an aura of controlled power. His piercing eyes scanned the assembly, acknowledging each member with a courteous nod. Leonora, stepping forward with grace, extended her hand. "Signor Bellini, it is an honour to host you."

Antonio, taking her hand, replied with a smile that didn't quite reach his eyes, "The pleasure is mine, Signora Morosini. Your estate is even grander than the tales suggest."

Leonora, ever the poised hostess, gestured towards the grandeur of the hall. "I trust your journey was comfortable?"

"Indeed," Antonio began, his voice smooth like velvet, "the roads to your illustrious estate are as welcoming as its residents." He caught Liliana's gaze for a split second, offering a sly, almost mischievous smile. "And the view upon arrival is unmatched in all of Venice."

Liliana, never one to shy away, retorted playfully, "It's often said that the Bellinis have an eye for beauty, though I've heard they are equally known for their strategic foresight in business. It must be quite a burden, carrying the weight of such a reputation."

Giovanni, observing the exchange, decided to join in. "I've heard tales of your recent expeditions, Signore Bellini. Rumours of treasures from the East, unparalleled in their allure. But surely, rumours are just... rumours."

"Ah, Signore Giovanni, the artist's curiosity is insatiable. Yes, the East holds many treasures, some visible, others hidden. But there are gems, even here in Venice, whose allure might rival those of the distance shores," Antonio said, giving a sly wink and a smile to Liliana.

Leonora interjected gracefully, "Indeed, Venice is a treasure trove in its own right. Our past, present, and future are entwined with tales of valour, love, and mystery. Perhaps, during your stay, we might share some of our own stories."

Antonio, his gaze flitting to the various faces surrounding him, replied, "I look forward to it, Signora. After all, a shared story is the beginning of many great legacies."

****

The grand doors of the dining hall opened, revealing a

room that felt as if it had been conjured from a dream. The chamber was bathed in a warm golden light, emanating from massive crystal chandeliers that hung from the frescoed ceiling, each depicting a chapter from Venetian history. Long tables adorned with silverware, crystal goblets, and porcelain plates gleamed beneath the radiance, while tall windows framed the serene views of Venice's tranquil canals. Each window was like a living painting, capturing a moment in the ever-evolving tapestry of Venice.

A soft melody, courtesy of a string quartet positioned in a cozy alcove, gently filled the room, every note playing homage to a city that danced between dreams and reality. The scent of roasting meats, fresh herbs, and exotic spices wafted through, promising a feast that was as much a journey for the senses as it was a culinary delight.

Antonio, ever the seasoned traveler, couldn't help but be momentarily entranced. He whispered to Leonora, "Your home rivals the tales of Eastern palaces I've heard, Signora. It is as if the walls echo the songs of bygone eras and the floors tread the paths of legends."

Leonora, gracefully accepting the compliment, responded, "We Morosinis believe in preserving our history and our tales, Signor Bellini. Every corner of this palazzo holds a story, a whisper of the past."

As the guests settled, servants flitted around like ethereal wraiths, their movements so synchronised it was as if they danced to a tune only they could hear. Course after course was presented, each dish an artwork, each flavour telling its own tale. From the fresh seafood caught from Venice's own lagoon to the rich stews and roasts, every bite was a testament to the culinary expertise of the Morosini household.

It was during the main course, as a sumptuous roasted peacock was being served, that Antonio, with a sip of his wine, cleared his throat. "Signora Morosini," he began, his voice measured, "as much as I revel in the delights of this evening, I must confess that my visit isn't purely social."

Leonora, her eyes sharp and discerning, responded, "We had anticipated as much, Signor Bellini. A man of your stature seldom travels without purpose."

Antonio smiled, acknowledging the point. "Indeed. While trade and wealth are cornerstones of the Bellini are, we also value alliances, relationships that strengthen both families involved." He paused, letting the implication hang in the air, before adding, "Marriage, as history has shown us, is often the most potent alliance of all."

Leonora, always the strategist, took a moment before replying, "The Morosini lineage is one of pride and honour. Any union we consider must ensure the prosperity and honour of both houses. Tell me, Signor Bellini, what do you believe such an alliance would bring?"

Antonio, leaning slightly forward, said "Beyond the obvious merging of wealth and influence, it's the union of two legacies, two stories that could shape the future of Venice. Together, our families could redefine trade, arts, and even politics."

Across the table, Liliana, her usual vibrant demeanour subdued, observed Antonio with an intensity borne of both curiosity, apprehension, and a sparked interest. Every gesture, every inflection in his voice, every concealed glance he cast her way - she absorbed it all, trying to decipher the man who might, by the whims of fate and family, become her life partner.

As dessert - a delicate panna cotta infused with rosewater and adorned with gold leaf - was served, Liliana decided to join the conversation. "Signor Bellini," she began, her voice soft yet confident, "you speak of unions and alliances, of combined legacies. But tell me, what of love? Does it find a place in these grand plans?"

Antonio, momentarily taken aback, met her gaze. There was a depth to his eyes, a sincerity that surprised her. "Signorina Liliana," he began, choosing his words carefully, "in the world of trade and politics, love is often a luxury, not a given. But it is also true that the most enduring of partnerships, the ones that stand the test of time and challenge, are built on mutual respect and understanding. And sometimes, in the most unexpected of moments, love finds its way."

The night wore on, filled the the gentle hum of conversation and the lingering melodies of the string quartet. As the last notes drifted away, the Morosini dining hall echoed with the contented sighs of a memorable evening in the heart of Venice.

****

The ornate chandeliers hanging from the ceilings cast warm, amber lights that illuminated the vast corridors of the Morosini Palazzo. As the guests rose from their seats, stretching their limbs and sharing pleasantries, Leonora, with the grace befitting the matriarch of the household, offered a tour of their treasured home.

"Signore Bellini," she began, her voice soft but commanding, "It would be a delight to show you our family's pride, to share with you the legacy built by the Morosinis over centuries."

Antonio nodded, "A tour of the famed Morosini Palazzo? It would be an honour."

They began in the main hall. A grand, sprawling space adorned with intricate mosaics that told tales of old, of brave Morosini ancestors setting sail for distant lands and the many treasures they'd amassed over the years. Every tile, every shade seemed to breathe life into these stories, making them almost palpable.

As they meandered through the hallways, Antonio's sharp eyes roved, taking in the stunning frescoes that adorned the walls. "You have a beautiful home. It tells tales of both time and love," he commented, a slight tilt to his voice.

Leonora smiled gracefully, "Thank you, Signor Bellini. Every corner, every brick, speaks of our family's journey."

Giovanni chimed in, eager to share his interests with the resplendent guest, "Signor Bellini, you seem to be a man with an interest in the pursuit of knowledge, allow me to show you our library. It's a haven for anyone with a love for history and the arts." And with a hand gently placed on Antonio's elbow, Giovanni steered him away.

The library was a masterpiece in itself. Floor-to-ceiling wooden shelves brimming with leather-bound books, the scent of aged parchment permeating the air. Rich draperies muted the sounds for outside, and a grand wooden desk sat at one end of the room, strewn with maps and ink pots.

"I've always been fond of libraries," Antonio remarked, his voice filled with genuine admiration. "There's something about being surrounded by knowledge, by tales penned down by hands long gone, that's deeply comforting."

Leonora, seizing the moment, added "Many of these are first editions, Signor Bellini. My ancestors had quite the penchant for collecting rare manuscripts."

They moved on, with Liliana leading the way to the grand ballroom. The sheer expanse of the room, with its gleaming marble floors reflecting the chandeliers above and tall arched windows offering views of the moonlit canals, was breathtaking.

Antonio took a moment, absorbing the room's grandeur. "You Morosinis certainly know how to leave an impression."

Liliana chuckled softly, "Our family has always believed in celebrating life, Signor Bellini. This ballroom has witnessed countless dances, masquerades, and celebrations."

Finally, as they stood on a balcony overlooking the serene waters of the canal, the silvery light of the moon casting reflections that danced on the water's surface, Antonio spoke, albeit with a hint of resignation.

"You have a magnificent home. It speaks volumes of your family's legacy. But I must admit, I came with an additional interest." Antonio shifted, his posture straightening. "With your permission, might I steal a moment with Signora Liliana by the canals? The beauty of Venice at night is best shared in good company."

Liliana, slightly taken aback but ever composed,

exchanged a brief, searching glance with her mother. Leonora, sensing an opportunity for insight, gave a subtle nod of approval.

The two descended the ornate stairway, making their way to the glistening canals that served as the lifeblood of Venice. The silhouette of Venice was truly a masterpiece under the moon's ethereal glow. Buildings of historic grandeur reflected on the shimmering waters, while soft, dulcet tones of the distant lute played a serenade that seemed composed solely for the city's nocturnal serenity.

Upon reaching the canals, Antonio offered Liliana his arm, which she hesitated but accepted. Together, they began a slow walk along the stone pathways, the rhythmic splash of the water against the boats providing a gentle background melody.

"You know," Antonio began, gazing deeply into Liliana's eyes, "Venice's beauty is unparalleled, but it's more than just the canals and sunsets. It's the moments, the whispers, the stolen glances… and of course, its enchanting residents."

Liliana looked back at him, a playful twinkle in her eyes. "Signor Bellini, are you speaking of Venice, or is this a sly reference to the tension between us?"

He chuckled softly, a light blush dusting his cheeks. "Ah, you're perceptive, Signora Liliana. Indeed, this pull, this… intrigue between us, has kindled a flame within me. But not in the way you might assume."

Her eyebrows arched delicately, her curiosity piqued. "Then do share your secrets."

Antonio hesitated for a moment, looking out at the canal. "In this city of love and mystery, I've met many enchanting souls. Yet, some connections... some sparks are rarer than others."

Liliana leaned in closer, her voice a gentle murmur, "Not every connection can be defined, Signor Bellini. Some feelings are best left unspoken, felt deeply within."

He turned toward her, the intensity in his gaze unmistakable. "This pull between us... it's not just fleeting. It feels like a journey, a shared destiny. Like two souls destined to intertwine."

She smiled coyly, her fingers lightly touching his arm. "And yet, the most passionate tales are often laced with danger and excitement. Stories of stolen glances, whispered confessions, and hearts racing."

Antonio smirked, drawing her closer, "Intrigue and romance are the lifeblood of Venice, are they not? But beneath every whisper, every stolen moment, there's an undeniable truth. Our connection isn't just a mere attraction, it's a bond waiting to be explored."

They continued their leisurely stroll, occasionally interrupted by passing gondoliers serenading their patrons with traditional Venetian songs. Antonio took a moment to secure a gondola for them, guiding Liliana onto the boat with a courteous hand.

As they glided through the serene waters, the city's allure wrapped around them. The ornate bridges, the historic palazzos, and the echoing laughter from nearby balconies intensified their budding connection.

"Tell me, Liliana," Antonio asked, his voice low and inviting, "what captures your heart in this city?"

She replied with a hint of mischief in her eyes, "The

allure of hidden corners, the whispers of past lovers, and the promise of secret rendezvous. Venice isn't just a place, it's an emotion."

He leaned closer, entranced, "And emotions are powerful, aren't they?"

She nodded, her voice softening, "Indeed, they are. But like the tides, they can ebb and flow. They can be intoxicating one moment and treacherous the next."

The evening deepened, their conversation weaving between tales of personal adventures, shared dreams, and light-hearted jests. They discussed art, music, and the timeless allure of Venice. Their rapport was undeniable, filling the spaces between them like a delicate melody.

As the gondola approached its destination, Antonio, filled with sincerity, murmured, "Liliana, I want you to understand that my intrigue in you is genuine. Every sentiment I've expressed is from the heart."

Liliana, every graceful, replied with a knowing smile, "Time will tell, Signor Bellini. In Venice, as with matters of the heart, what appears serene above can hide passionate depths beneath."

They disembarked, their conversation's resonance still fresh, as Venice continued to envelop them in its romantic glow.

****

The pathways of Venice, with their worn cobblestones, told tales of countless footsteps, of whispered secrets, of fateful encounters. It was upon one such path that Giovanni, immersed in the world within his sketchbook, chanced upon a scene that caught his artistic eye. Yet, it wasn't the aesthetic that held him, but the participants of the tableau: his sister Liliana and Antonio Bellini.

Their profiles were illuminated by the luminescent glow of the lanterns hanging from nearby residences. Shadows danced upon their faces, creating a chiaroscuro that would have fascinated any artist. But for Giovanni, the play of light and dark held a more personal intrigue. The intimacy of their conversation, the proximity in which they stood, the intensity of Antonio's gaze - it all sent a ripple of unease through him.

Closing his sketchbook, Giovanni approached them, his stride confident yet nonchalant. "Signor Bellini, my sister," he greeted with a casual tilt of his head, "I hope the evening treats you well. The canals have a way of amplifying moonlight, don't they?"

Antonio replied smoothly, "Indeed, Signor Giovanni. It's as if the city itself conspires to add to its allure."

Giovanni's gaze fitted between them, observing the subtle dynamics, the unsaid words that seemed to hang in the cool evening air. "I find the canals most inspiring at this hour," he commented, opening his sketchbook and showing a half-finished drawing of the moonlit waters. "The play of the shadows, the reflection of the stars - it's almost ethereal."

Liliana, sensing the tension but playing along, added, "Giovanni has always been a dreamer. Always lost in his sketches, finding beauty in the mundane."

Giovanni, while appreciating the compliment, didn't miss a beat, "Speaking of which, Liliana, I've been meaning to discuss the portrait I wish to paint of you. Perhaps now is as good a time as any?"

Antonio's eyes sharpened just a fraction, sensing the shift in dynamics. "A portrait? Sounds fascinating. Will I be included, I wonder?"

Giovanni's eyes met Antonio's a silent challenge passing between them. "The composition is yet to be decided. But it will capture the essence of the subject, as all good portraits should."

The unspoken duel of words continued, each man measuring the other, gauging strengths and intentions. The beauty of Venice around them stood in stark contrast to the brewing storm of their conversation.

As they walked, the sounds of the city at night played a gently lullaby - the distant crooning of a serenader, the soft splash of water against stone, the murmur of conversations from nearby cafes. Palazzos, with their grand arches and intricate stonework, stood silent to witness to centuries of history.

Liliana, ever perceptive, interjected, hoping to diffuse the situation, "Antonio, have you seen our family's private gallery? It holds paintings from several generations, each telling a tale of its own."

Giovanni, seizing the opportunity, added, "Yes, it's a testament to our lineage. But the gallery is not just about the art; it's about the stories behind each canvas."

And so, the trio made their way back to the Morosini estate, the atmosphere laden with both the weight of unspoken words and the potential of what the future might hold. As they entered the grand hallway, the flicker of torchlight case dancing shadows, creating a tapestry of light and dark that seemed to mirror the intricate dance of their relationships.

Inside the gallery, walls adorned with portraits and landscapes silently watched the trio. Each painting, a frozen moment in time, held within its frame stories of love, loss, and legacy. The gently play of candlelight revealed the intimate details of each artwork, casting a warm glow upon their faces. Surrounded by the chronicles of their ancestors, the atmosphere was one of reverence and reflection.

Antonio, sensing the evening had drawn to its natural conclusion, gently folded his hands behind him. "Signor Giovanni, Signorina Liliana, this evening has been both enlightening and enchanting. I must take my leave, for the hour grows late, and the city in all its beauty beckons me to its embrace."

Giovanni stepped forward. "Signor Bellini, it has been a pleasure hosting you, and as you journey through the city's streets, may Venice treat you as kindly as you have treated us this evening."

With a slight nod and a smile that held a myriad of emotions, Antonio turned to depart. His entourage, ever watchful, followed suit, their footsteps echoing softly in the corridors of the Morosini estate.

Once the sounds of their departure faded, the grandeur of the palazzo seemed to close in on the Morosinis. They found themselves in the main salon, a room of velvet drapes, intricate woodwork, and grand chandeliers that dangled like crystalline constellations.

Leonora, her countenance a mix of grace and gravitas,

spoke first. "This alliance, it promises much. The wealth, influence, and status it brings could elevate our family to unparalleled heights."

Leonora pondered, the soft flicker of candlelight casting an ephemeral glow on her face. "Every individual has layers, desires, dreams. It is our task to discern if aligning with Antonio's aspirations benefits the Morosini legacy."

Giovanni moved closer to a window, the luminous reflection of moonlit canals painting a serene image on the glass. "It isn't just about legacy. It's about ensuring our family's safety, its future."

The room seemed to breathe with them, the weight of decisions, potential futures, and ancestral expectations making the walls pulse with a silent urgency. The murmur of the city outside, with its distant laughter, gently lapping of canal waters, and far-off melodies, seemed to be a world away.

Leonora, finally breaking the heavy introspection, whispered more to herself than to her children, "Decisions of this magnitude demands clarity and foresight." Moving towards an ornate mirror, she gazed at her reflection. The woman staring back was a matriarch, a pillar of strength, her eyes pools of wisdom and determination.

Giovanni, placing a gentle hand on his sister's shoulder, mused, "The crossroads we stand upon is one of many we will face. Our choices, influenced by both heart and mind, will pen the chapters of our family's story."

Liliana responded softly, "And we will all face them, together."

As the night deepened, the Morosini family, bound by

blood and shared purpose, found solace in their unity. The palazzo, with its silent walls and echoing corridors, stood testament to their lineage. Leonora, her silhouette framed by the grandeur of the room, remained deep in thought, the decisions of tomorrow resting on the resolve of today.

Chapter 3

Dawn broke over Venice, and with its first golden rays, the Serenissima stirred from her nocturnal repose. The sun's gentle embrace reflected off the canals, turning them into shimmering tapestries of azure and gold. Gondolas, their elegant prows cutting through the calm waters, painted a scene straight from a master's canvas.

The Rialto market sprang to life. Fishmongers yelled their morning chants, presenting their fresh catch, scales glinting like newly minted coins. Spice merchants opened large wooden chests, releasing fragrances that would seduce even the most frugal of passersby. Rich aromas of cinnamon, cardamom, and cloves danced in the air, inviting, tempting and beckoning to all. Meanwhile, the fabric sellers unrolled silks and velvets, their luxurious surfaces catching the morning light and making them appear as though they'd been dipped in the very essence of the rainbow.

Yet, amid this panoply of sights, sounds, and scents, there was another layer to Venice that morning - a subtle, whispered undercurrent. Among the din and calmer, if one strained their ears, they could discern the murmurs, the soft exchanges of words passed like a secret lover's note under the table.

In the shade of an arched bridge, two masked women, draped in flowing brocades, exchanged hushed words. One whispered, her eyes darting, "Have you seen the Morosini palazzo lately? Such opulence! Such parties! One wonders where such fortune blossoms overnight." The other, a fan poised before her lips, replied with a coy smile, "Intrigue and secrets, my dear. Every stone in Venice could tell a tale."

In a lavishly adorned salon of a Venetian noble's residence, plump on gilded cushions, gentlemen with well-trimmed beards and ladies in elaborate headdresses sipped the finest wines. Their chatter, like a soft symphony, rose and fell. But interspersed were pointed questions. "Have you dined with the Morosinis recently? It's said their silverware is now edged with gold!" Another remarked, "A little bird told me their recent endeavours in trade have been... astonishingly fruitful."

A street musician, strumming a lute, played for the market-goers, but his ears were not deaf to the discourse of the crowd. As coins clinked into his hat, he overheard a merchant say, "The Morosinis, ah! Their galleons dock heavy and leave light. Prosperity seems to favor them at every turn."

Even as children played tag through the labyrinthine alleyways, their innocent laughter echoing, snippets of their parents' conversations had found their way into their games. "You be the rich Morosini, and I'll be the Duke!" one shouted, his little velvet cape fluttering behind him.

In the distance, the great bell of St. Mark's tolled, its sonorous chimes flowing over the city, as if to remind everyone of the inexorable march of time. The Doge's Palaces, its Gothic spires reaching skyward, watched over the city like a sentinel. But its stones, if they could speak, would tell of the countless whispered secrets they'd absorbed over centuries.

Venice, in her ageless beauty, continued her dance between light and shadow, truth and rumour. The Serenissima, ever the heater of intrigue, was abuzz with the tale of the Morosini family. And as the day wore on, these murmurs would grow, turning into stories, tales, and legends, woven into the rich tapestry of Venetian life.

Giovanni Morosini, with a feathered quill tucked behind his ear and a parchment under his arm, strolled down the sun-dappled pathways of the city. The artist in him was perpetually on a quest, seeking inspiration in every mosaic, every ivy-laden balcony, and every reflection that danced upon the serene waters of the canals.

As he entered Campo San Polo, the largest square in Venice, he admired the frescoes that adorned nearby structures, each telling tales of heroics, love, and tragedy. The square buzzed with energy, as artists sketched, poets recited their verses, and musicians serenaded passersby with lilting tunes. It was here that Giovanni hoped to find the most vibrant of colours for his palette - colours that breathed life into the tales he painted.

Yet, as he was engrossed in conversation with a pigment seller, his ears caught the mellifluous straits of a conversation not intended for him. Just a few steps away, behind a facade of potted ferns and cascading wisteria, a trio of masked nobles stood, their velvets rustling and fans fluttering.

"You know, I've heard tales," began the first, a tall figure draped in burgundy, his mask adorned with a plume of peacock feathers. "Tales of the Morosini's cellars, now brimming with wines that even the French would covet."

The second, a lady whose azure gown shimmered like the midday sea, her mask embellished with crystals that caught the sun, chimed in. "And their parties! Ah, the grandeur, the opulence! It's as if every star from the heavens has descended into their ballroom."

Giovanni discreetly angled his body towards them, feigning interest in a pot of cerulean blue pigment, but straining his ears to catch every syllable.

The third, his mask simpler but his robe richly embroidered with threads of gold, added, "It is said that their coffers are now so heavy, they had to reinforce the floors of their treasury."

The lady laughed, her voice like the tinkling of wind chimes. "Oh, come now! Surely you jest. But I've indeed heard whispers about an heirloom - a gem so exquisite, it could make the moon pale with envy."

The tall noble interjected, "Ah, but where did it come from? How did the Morosinis, respected but never exorbitantly wealthy, come into such good fortune?"

Giovanni's heart thudded louder, each beat resonating with a mixture of pride and concern. The weight of the sapphire's legend and its allure on Venice's elite was becoming palpable. As the trio continued their discussion, speculating on trades, alliances, and even alleged dark deals, Giovanni felt the fabric of the Morosini legacy being toyed with, stretched and embroidered with tales and fancies.

Seeing an opportunity, Giovanni approached them, his voice steady but tinged with a hint of playfulness. "Ah, Signores, Signora, it seems my family's name graces your lips this fine morning. As a Morosini, might I quench your curiosities with truths, rather than let them be drenched in tavern tales?"

The three exchanged glances, their eyes, the only visible part of their faces, widening in surprise. The lady, with a coy tilt of her head, replied, "Ah, Signor Morosini! Forgive our idle chatter. Venice, in her grandeur, does love her stories. And your family, it seems, has become the protagonist of many."

Giovanni bowed slightly, his eyes never leaving theirs. "Every mosaic has its tales, Signora. Some real, some imagined. It is the beholder who must discern the truth." With a knowing smile, he bid them farewell, leaving the trio in a pool of shared glances and whispered words.

Giovanni walked the length of the Grand Canal, letting the sights and sounds of the city wash over him. The dome of Santa Maria della Salute shimmered in the afternoon sun, and gondoliers navigated their vessels with a grace that spoke of centuries of tradition. Yet, for Giovanni, the city's allure was not just in its magnificent facades and winding waterways, but in the stories whispered amongst its inhabitants, stories that now encompassed his own family.

Meanwhile, across the city in a sunlit piazza fringed with budding oleanders and adorned with the soft play of water from a marble fountain, Liliana Morosini found herself amidst an opulent gathering. Arched walkways lined the square, their shadows offering respite from the sun. Musicians played gentle tunes, their melodies intertwining with the laughter and chatter that filled the air.

Ladies in flowing gowns of silk and satin twirled fans, their vibrant colours a testament to the city's love for life and artistry. Gentlemen in brocade vests and feathered hats discussed politics, trades, and of course, the ever-intriguing rise of certain families in Venetian society.

Liliana, dressed in a gown of soft lavender that complemented her raven-black hair, stood as a beacon of attention. She was approached by a flurry of acquaintances, each eager to offer their felicitations.

"Signorina Morosini!" exclaimed Contessa Blanca, a woman known for her extensive collection of Venetian masks. "What a delightful surprise to see you here. Your family's recent festivities are the talk of the town. Such extravagance, such style! Venice has not seen the likes in many a season."

Liliana offered a gracious smile, "Thank you, Contessa. We are simply celebrating life's blessings."

As the afternoon waned, a cavalcade of other well-wishers approached Liliana. Some, like Signor De Luca, a respected scholar, offered genuine warmth. "My dear Liliana," he said, eyes twinkling, "Seeing the Morosini family flourish warms an old man's heart. Venice needs families with integrity at its helm."

However, not all were as forthright as the good scholar. Among the genuine well-wishers were those who concealed their true intentions beneath layers of faux admiration. Like Signora Grimaldi, a lady with a penchant for gossip, whose honeyed words were often laced with venom. "Liliana, darling," she crooned, her eyes narrowing with a hint of mischief, "Every corner of Venice echoes with tales of the Morosini prosperity. And that heirloom, my dear, is said to be the very heart of the ocean. How fortunate you are!"

Liliana, trained in the delicate ballet of Venetian diplomacy, replied, "Fortunate, Signora Grimaldi, is but a moment's breeze. We cherish our history and our present, for they mold our tomorrow."

The sun, once bright and imposing, now cast long shadows, heralding the approach of dusk. As the gathering drew to a close, and guests began to take their leave, Liliana felt both drained and invigorated. The attention, both genuine and feigned, was a testament to her family's evolving position in the tapestry of Venetian society.

As she stepped onto a waiting gondola, the gentle lap of water against wood and the distant toll of church bells accompanied her thoughts. Venice, with its shimmering canals and labyrinthine alleys, was a city of masks - not just the ornate ones worn during its famed carnival, but the invisible ones worn every day, hiding intentions, dreams, and sometimes, envy.

****

Tucked away in an unassuming corner, the 'Taverna al Gatto Nero' stood as a silent witness to the city's countless secrets. Overlooking a narrow canal, its stone walls were darkened by time and the salty lagoon air. On this particular evening, its dimly lit interiors were bustling with a mixed clientele - sailors fresh from a sea voyage, merchants discussing their day's profits, and locals seeking solace in a glass of wine or two.

A trio of elderly men occupied a corner table, their voices barely audible above the din. Their conversation, however, stood out amidst the common tavern banter.

"Have you heard, Pietro? About the Morosinis and their prized possession?" asked Mercurio, his eyes darting around to ensure they weren't overheard.

Pietro, his face etched with wrinkles, leaned in, "Ah, you mean the sapphire. They say it's not just a jewel, but a talisman. Some say it's the very reason for their sudden prosperity."

Giuseppe, the third of the group, scoffed, "Tales and nothing more. The Morosinis have always been shrewd. It's just business acumen."

But Mercurio wasn't convinced. "They were doing well, yes. But this? This sudden rise? It's not just about being shrewd. That gem has power. Old Benedetta says it's been blessed by the saints. And you know she's rarely wrong."

The talk of the sapphire would have remained just that - talk - had it not been for a shadowy figure seated at the bar. Draped in a cloak, with only his piercing eyes visible beneath the hood, he seemed more interested in his drink than in the conversation around him. But appearances, especially in Venice, could be deceptive.

Eavesdropping on the old men's conversation, the mysterious man summoned the barmaid, placing a few coins on the counter. "Another for the road, bella," he murmured, his voice smooth yet carrying an undertone of menace. As she poured the wine, he leaned in, "Tell me, signorina, what do you know of the Morosini's sapphire?"

She hesitated, "Only what everyone says. It's a beautiful gem, and some believe it brings good fortune."

He smirked, "Just good fortune? Or something… more?"

She lowered her voice, leaning in, "Well, there are tales. That it's a talisman. Blessed by saints, cursed by the devil, or maybe both. But who believes in such tales?"

The man's eyes twinkled with mischief, "Tales often hold a kernel of truth, bella. Remember that." Leaving a generous tip, he melted into the night.

****

The next evening, in 'La Rosa Rossa', another tavern several streets away, the same cloaked figure was seen regaling an audience with tales of the powerful sapphire that could grant wishes and change destinies. And as the days went by, the stories grew in magnitude and detail, with every retelling adding another layer to the sapphire's legend.

The taverns and squares of Venice, already abuzz with chatter about the Morosini family's ascent, now found a more tantalising topic of discussion. The enigmatic man, whether by design or accident, had sown the seeds of a myth that took root into the very heart of Venetian society.

Wine vendors, fishmongers, and craftsmen spoke of it in hushed tones. Children playing by the canals wove stories of the gem's magical powers. And as the sun set each day, casting its golden hue on the Serenissima's shimmering waters, the sapphire's allure grew, casting a spell on the city, making it question the boundaries between reality and the mystical. Amidst the swirling rumours and embellished tales, the shadowy figure remained elusive. But his presence was felt, like a soft silver bell or a breeze before a storm, stirring the waters of the city.

****

Within the grand halls of the Morosini estate, sumptuous drapes of red velvet and golden thread flowed like riverbeds. Exquisite paintings showcasing the achievements of generations past told of a legacy both grand and enduring. Gilded chandeliers hung from the ceiling, their flames dancing merrily, sending golden reflections skimming across the marble floors.

However, the aura of luxury was punctuated with a palpable tension that evening.

Leonora, resplendent in her evening gown of sapphire blue, stood by a grand window, her silhouette framed by the crescent moon's glow. The very jewel that was the topic of Venice's whispered conversations rested upon her delicate neck, its deep blue hue seemingly absorbing the silvery luminescences of the moonlight.

Her heart, usually as still as the placid waters of a lagoon, now beat with a rapidity that echoed her growing unease. She had always been attuned to the symphony of Venice; its every murmur, sigh, and exclamation never escaped her acute senses. And now, its current song - a curious mix of admiration, envy, and burgeoning superstition - had her deeply concerned.

Every compliment bestowed upon her at gatherings seemed to have a hidden untertone, every gaze lingering a tad too long on the sapphire. Even the laughter of children playing in the streets seemed to hide tales of the gem's magical prowess.

Drawing a deep breath to calm her racing heart, she summoned the captain of her guard, a robust man named Lorenzo, known for his unwavering loyalty to the Morosini family. "Lorenzo," she began, her voice a soft caress yet unmistakably firm, "I need you to double the guard during the night. Especially around the southern wing. And no one, absolutely no one, is to be allowed entry without my express permission."

Lorenzo bowed, "It shall be done, my lady."

She held his gaze, ensuring he understood the gravity of her instructions. "We live in uncertain times, Lorenzo. Trust is a luxury we can ill afford. The city's alleys are abuzz with tales, tales that may draw unwanted attention to our home."

Leonora, always a paragon of grace and composure, now felt the weight of the world upon her. The sapphire, once a symbol of their family's proud lineage, now felt like a beacon, drawing both the genuinely curious and the potentially nefarious.

She began wearing the heirloom more frequently, not just as a mark of her family's prestige, but as a silent proclamation of her intent to guard it with her life. The jewel, with its deep blue depths, became an extension of her very soul. Its cool surface against her skin served as both a comfort and a constant reminder of the tales weaving their way through the Venetian nights.

****

The serene night enveloped the Morosini estate in a gentle embrace, but inside, the atmosphere was charged with anticipation. In a private chamber, a room adorned with tapestries showcasing landscapes from far-off lands, Leonora sat at the head of an ornate table, its mahogany surface gleaming in the dim light. Flanking her were Giovanni and Liliana, their expressions a blend of curiosity and concern.

Leonora began, her voice steady but tinged with a gravity that instantly commanded attention, "My dearest ones, we find ourselves at the confluence of opportunity and vulnerability. The murmurs that ripple through the city have begun to shape perceptions, casting shadows where there was once only light."

Giovanni, his mind always inclined towards strategy and logic, leaned forward, his fingers steepled in contemplation. "If the city believes us to be rising, why not ride this wave, Mother? Rumours, after all, are like the wind. We cannot control their origin, but we can set out sails to make the most of them. Perhaps it's time we sought alliances, intertwined our fortunes with other illustrious families, thereby solidifying our place in the city's tapestry."

Leonora listened intently, her eyes reflecting the deep reservoirs of wisdom she had accumulated over the years. She then shifted her gaze to Liliana, who had remained silent, absorbing the weight of the conversation.

Liliana's voice, when she spoke, had the lyrical quality of a soft rain, gentle yet persistent. "While Giovanni's strategy holds merit, we must tread with care. We are the custodians of a rich heritage, one that extends beyond gemstones and treasures. The sapphire is but a chapter in our story, not the entire tale. We mustn't let it overshadow who we are, our values, and the legacy we wish to leave behind."

Leonora nodded in agreement, her heart swelling with pride at the profound insights of her children. "Both of you bring forth valid perspectives. Giovanni, your pragmatism has always been our anchor, guiding us through threaterous waters with unerring precision. And Liliana, your wisdom reminds us that while the physical realm has its allure, it's the intangible - honour, love, legacy - that truly defines us."

Giovanni, ever attuned to the nuances of power dynamics, added, "If we are to align with other families, it must be a union of mutual respect and shared vision. Not just an opportunistic alignment birthed from the crucible of rumours."

Liliana softly interjected, "And in these unions, let us remember to be ourselves. The sapphire may be our companion, but it is not our compass. We navigate our path."

Leonora, taking a moment to absorb the wisdom emanating from her offspring, concluded, "Very well. We shall approach these alliances with both caution and sincerity. But always, always we shall be guided by the ethos that has been the bedrock of our lineage. Our name shall echo not just with affluence, but with integrity." The trio sat in reflective silence for a moment, united in purpose, bound by blood, and fortified by the shared vision of a legacy that transcended material wealth. The night outside was still.

****

Beyond the palatial confines of the Morosini estate, the

world went about its rhythms, and so did Leonora. Her routine visits to the church were both a respite and a time of reflection. The church, standing tall since time immemorial, was a marvel of architecture. Its stones were seasoned by time, and its spires reached for the heavens with an elegance that spoke of epochs gone by.

Upon entering, the first sensation that always greeted Leonora was the church's quiet grandeur. Colossal pillars, wreathed in histories and secrets, held aloft the domed ceiling adorned with frescoes depicting tales of faith and valour. The scent of burning incense danced in the air, its tendrils weaving intricate patterns, like the very breath of the Divine.

She slowly made her way to a pew, the hushed whispers of her steps echoing in the cavernous expanse. Settling down, she inhaled deeply, letting the sanctity of the place envelop her. It was in these moments of solitude that Leonora often found her clarity, the murmurs of the world silenced by the profound stillness.

As she was lost in her thoughts, a rustle from a neighbouring pew drew her attention. Turning her head subtly, her eyes met those of a woman. Shrouded in layers of dark fabric, only her eyes were visible, piercing and ageless, set in a face concealed by a veil. The woman, with a grace that seemed out of place, approached Leonora.

Without any preamble, her voice, reminiscent of a forgotten melody, whispered, "Prosperity shines bright, but shadows loom. Protect what is yours."

Leonora, though a woman of formidable mettle, felt a momentary shiver, like a winter breeze stealing into a warm room. "Who are you?" she asked, her voice steady despite the mysteriousness of the encounter.

The veiled woman merely tilted her head, the corners of her eyes crinkling in what might have been a smile. "In this vast tapestry of existence, I am but a single thread, weaving in and out of stories, binding fates. Remember my words, Lady Morosini."

Before Leonora could question further, the enigmatic woman turned, her silhouette fading into the dappled light filtering through the stained glass. It was as if the very air had swallowed her, leaving behind only the resonance of her cryptic words.

Leonora sat motionless, the weight of the encounter pressing upon her. The church, which had always been her sanctuary, now bore witness to this peculiar rendezvous. Gathering herself, she rose, her every movement a ballet of grace and determination. As she made her way out, the tales depicted in the frescoes seemed to whisper to her, their voices merging with the echo of the veiled woman's words.

Emerging into the world outside, Leonora was greeted by the embrace of nature. Birds flitted about, their songs composing an aria of life. Trees swayed gently, their leaves rustling like the pages of a well-read book. The sun, its golden rays painting everything in a warm hue, stood sentinel in the azure sky.

Yet, for all the beauty around her, Leonora's mind was ensnared by the web of mystery the veiled woman had spun. "Protect what is yours." The phrase resonated, its meaning both clear and obscured.

As she made her way back to the Morosini estate, the

world around her seemed to hold its breath, watching, waiting. The journey back was punctuated by moments of reflection, the landscape around her an ever-changing canvas of life's intricacies.

****

Giovanni's art studio was a sanctum of creativity, nestled deep within the Morosini estate. From floor to ceiling, the room bore testament to his prodigious talent. Canvasses of various sizes, some finished in exquisite detail and others mere strokes of inspiration, lined the walls. Each painting was a symphony of colour, a dance of light and shadow. The smell of oil paint and turpentine hung in the air, creating an atmosphere of perpetual artistic fervour.

On this particular evening, Giovanni sat hunched over a canvas, the soft glow from the candles painting his features in an amber hue. His hands, stained with colour, moved deftly, their motions fluid and confident. His brush danced, creating strokes that brought forth imagery both vivid and ethereal. A pot of ink lay by his side, its contents a wellspring for his quill that sketched outlines with meticulous precision.

Time seemed to halt in this cocoon of creativity. Outside, the world slept, blanketed by the shroud of night, but inside, Giovanni's world was awash with hues and textures. His concentration was unparalleled, a communion between artist and art, spirit and canvas.

However, a faint whisper, almost imperceptible, punctured this serenity. Giovanni stilled, his ears pricking up. The whisper grew louder, resembling the murmurs of cloaked conversations, clandestine and secretive. It seemed to emanate from just outside his window.

Laying down his brush, he approached the window cautiously. Drawing the heavy drapes apart, he peered into the moonlit garden. The silver glow illuminated the meticulously maintained hedges and statues, casting elongated shadows that played tricks on the eyes.

For a brief moment, all seemed ordinary. But then, out of the corner of his eye, he caught a fleeting movement - a shadow, swift and silent, darting away from the window's glow. It moved with an agility that belied its intent, disappearing into the intricate pathways of the garden, its trace lost in the network of flora and stone.

Giovanni's pulse quickened. Intruders were rare in the Morosini estate, especially with the heightened security Leonora had recently mandated. Could it be a mere gardener, or perhaps one of the newer guards unfamiliar with his nocturnal habits? But instinct told him otherwise.

He hastily donned a robe, its fabric whispering against the floor as he made his way downstairs. The grand staircase, usually radiant in the daylight, now felt like a cavernous descent into the unknown. Each step echoed with a sense of purpose, mingling with the rhythmic ticking of the grand clock, which stood as a sentinel to the passage of time.

Once in the garden, the fragrances of nocturnal blossoms greeted him - the heady scent of moonflowers and the sweet perfume of night-blooming jasmine. The night's stillness was palpable, broken only by the distant hoot of an owl and the gentle rustle of leaves in the evening breeze.

Despite the serenity, Giovanni, couldn't shake off the feeling of being watched. His gaze flitted from one shadow to the next, trying to discern any abnormality, any hint of the intruder's presence. Minutes felt like hours as he ventured deeper, the moon his only companion, casting a silvery sheen over everything.

A soft crunch of gravel to his left made him whirl around. But it was just a nightingale, its feathers shimmering in the moonlight, taking flight from a nearby stone bench. Its song, usually a source of solace for Giovanni, now added to the night's enigmatic ambience.

He decided to explore the far end of the garden, where a beautiful marble fountain stood. Its waters, under the night's embrace, shimmered like a mirror reflecting the cosmos. As he neared it, he noticed something odd - a fresh set of footprints, moist against the dry path, leading toward the garden's exit.

It was clear that someone had indeed been here, their intentions as yet unknown. With a heavy heart and a mind swirling with questions, Giovanni, made his way back to the palazzo, determined to discuss the night's events come morning. In his studio, the candlelight continued its dance, casting a golden aura around the room.

****

The golden light of dawn streamed into the opulent chambers of the Morosini estate. Draped silks shimmered and the intoxicating aroma of fresh flowers permeated the rooms. This morning, a palpable tension enveloped the house, the previous night's unsettling events still fresh in their minds.

Giovanni, despite the restlessness that kept him awake, had summoned the family for an urgent meeting in the grand salon. The air in the salon was heavy with expectation, the soft glow from the crystal chandeliers above casting prismatic rainbows across the ornate walls.

Liliana, a beacon of grace, entered first, her gown flowing behind her like a river of silk. Giovanni, his face drawn but resolute, stood at the head of the room, while Leonora, poised and regal, took her place, her innate authority evident.

"We find ourselves at a crossroads," began Giovanni, his voice steady despite the undercurrent of concern. "There are whispers in every corner, shadows in broad daylight. It's imperative we make a firm stand."

Leonora nodded, her sharp eyes catching every nuance. "A demonstration," she mused, "a resounding declaration that the Morosini family is unyielding and resolute. We should consider hosting an event, perhaps?"

Liliana's eyes sparkled at the idea, "A grand ball, Mother! A grand ball unlike any Venice has seen in decades. Let the music play, let the wine flow, and let our state be filled with laughter and dance."

The thought of such a celebration was tantalising. It would be an assertion of their stature, a feast for the senses, showcasing the splendour and opulence they possessed. More importantly, it would silence the whispers, at least for a time, replacing them with awe and admiration.

"The preparations would be colossal," noted Giovanni,

rubbing his chin thoughtfully. "We would need the finest musicians, the most delectable dishes, and an ambiance that radiates magnificence."

"And guests," interjected Liliana, "Guests from every stratum of society. From nobility to artisans, let all see the grandeur of the Morosini family."

Leonora added, "This ball, while a celebration, will also serve as an opportunity. An opportunity to forge alliances, to nurture friendships, and to demonstrate our unwavering unity."

The trio, each in their own world of thoughts, pondered the grandiosity of the task ahead. From the scent of fresh roses to the gentle sway of waltzing couples, every detail would be meticulously planned.

"Costumes," mused Liliana, "Gowns and suits that shimmer and shine, capturing the essence of a night under the stars."

"We'll need to send out invitations," Giovanni added, "crafted with precision, bearing the emblem of our family. Each card an art piece, setting the tone for the evening."

"The gardens," Leonora whispered, lost in thought, "Lanterns, twinkling like the cosmos, guiding guests through a wonderland of blossoms and magic."

As the morning sun climbed higher, painting the room in a golden hue, the vision for the grand ball began to crystallise. Lists were made, tasks were assigned, and the Morosini estate was soon abuzz with activity.

Outside the grand salon, the staff, having caught wind of the upcoming event, were already in a flurry of excitement. Seamstresses were called upon to discuss fabrics and designs, chefs were consulted about the menu, and musicians from across the land were sought.

Giovanni sketched out a vision for the ballroom, imagining cascades of flowers hanging from the ceiling, creating a celestial ambiance. Liliana, with her innate sense of style, envisioned a theme - 'Night Under the Stars' - a celebration of the cosmos and the mysteries it held.

Leonora, meanwhile, had already begun penning the list of invitees, ensuring that the guests list was both diverse and influential. With each name she wrote, she envisaged alliances being forged, relationships being nurtured, and the standing of the Morosini family being solidified in the annals of history.

By evening, as the sun bid adieu, casting the world in hues of lavender and rose, the Morosini family sat back, their vision for the grand ball taking shape, ready to carve a night of enchantment into the heart of the city.

The grand ball, though days away, was already creating ripples of excitement. The anticipation was palpable, the promise of a night of splendour and elegance beckoning all. And as the city retired for the night, dreams of waltzes, sparkling gowns, and euphoric melodies danced in their minds.

****

The golden crescent of the waxing moon bathed the world in a luminescent sheen, casting ethereal shadows on cobblestoned streets and ancient architecture. As the cool night breeze danced with the delicate curtains, Leonora, clad in a cloak of deep cerulean, set out for a discreet part of the city. Her steps, though determined, bore the weight of a heart laden with concern.

She navigated through the narrow streets, leaving behind the grandeur of her palatial home, and entering into the realms where age-old wisdom dwelt. This part of the city was untouched by time; the buildings stood tall and proud, whispering tales form an age gone by. The hush of the night was occasionally broken by the distant hoot of an owl, a sentinel of the twilight realm.

It was here that the famed seer, Signora Seraphina, resided. Her abode was a modest structure with stone walls laden with ivy and moss. A vintage brass knocker, shaped like an owl, adorned her wooden door. With a deep breath, Leonora knocked thrice.

The door opened to reveal an aged woman, her silver hair cascading down like a shimmering waterfall, her eyes deep pools of wisdom that had seen countless sunrises and sunsets. Signora Seraphina's presence was both comforting and intimidating. She welcomed Leonora with a nod and a knowing smile, as if expecting her arrival.

"Signora Morosini," she greeted in a voice that was a soft blend of the rustling of autumn leaves and the gentle hum of a lullaby. "I sensed a perturbed spirit. Come, sit."

The interiors of Seraphina's haven were a reflection of her spirit - walls adorned with tapestries depicting celestial bodies, tables strewn with crystal balls, tarot decks, and ancient scrolls. Candles, emitting a soft lavender fragrance, were the sole sources of light, casting flickering shadows that seemed to dance to a tune only they could hear.

Leonora, taking a seat opposite the seer, began, "Signora Seraphina, recent events have unsettled me. I come seeking insight, hoping to find clarity in the mists of uncertainty."

The seer closed her eyes for a brief moment, her brow furrowing as if tapping into energies unseen. Then, with a fluid motion, she spread her tarot cards in a crescent shape, urging Leonora to draw three.

As the cards were revealed - The Moon, The Tower, and The Empress - Signora Seraphina's gaze deepened, reading the symbols and patterns that emerged.

"The Moon," she began, "suggests confusion, illusions, and the unconscious. It's a card of intuition and psychic forces." Her fingers traced the image of the moon on her card, her voice a meditative hum. "The Tower," she continued, "is a card of upheaval. It warns of sudden change, chaos. But from that chaos can emerge clarity, rebuilding." The image of a tower struck by lightning stared back at Leonora. Finally, she touched The Empress card, "A symbol of femininity, fertility, beauty, and nature. It represents a nurturing spirit and the material abundance of the earth."

Piecing the narrative together, Signora Seraphina locked eyes with Leonora, "Your family is on the cusp of significant change. While prosperity and abundance are evident, there are forces, both seen and unseen, that threaten your tranquility. Lean into your maternal instincts, protect and nurture what is dear."

Leonora, absorbing the seer's words, felt a strange amalgamation of unease and empowerment. She clutched her cloak, feeling the weight of responsibility, of her family's legacy and the path they tread.

"Remember," Seraphina whispered, her voice fading as if carried away by the wind, "in darkness, seek the light within. Trust your instincts, and in moments of doubt, let love guide you."

Thanking the seer, Leonora made her way back, the journey seeming shorter, her steps lighter. The words of Seraphina echoed in her mind, not as a dire warning, but as a beacon, urging her to be the protector, the guiding light for her family in times of obscurity.

Chapter 4

Under the embrace of twilight, the world shifted its colours. The indigo sky above weaved a tapestry, where stars began to shyly peek through, and the last rays of the sun cast long, golden fingers across the world. Giovanni, with the hood of his cloak pulled low, sought the sanctuary of the less trodden paths. Shadows played on the cobblestones, dancing and retreating as the occasional lantern threw its soft, wavering light. Each step he took was deliberate, ensuring his silhouette melted into the velvet darkness.

The city, with all its grandeur and vibrancy, also housed secrets; secrets whispered behind closed doors, sealed with hurried glances, and protected by the sanctity of the night. For Giovanni, these meandering alleys, which turned and twisted like the intricate strokes of an artist's brush, held the key to his own clandestine refuge.

Old brick walls stood like silent guardians, their surfaces weathered by time, bearing witness to countless stories. The soft chatter from the main streets faded, replaced by the hushed serenades of night creatures and the distant murmur of the canals. A cat, its coat a sleek obsidian, paused in its nocturnal hunt to assess Giovanni with luminescent eyes before darting away, a shadow chasing shadows.

Finally, he reached the familiar, secluded courtyard, its heart adorned with a fountain. The water bubbled gently, each droplet catching the moon's silvery sheen, creating ripples that played with the light in an endless, mesmerising dance. Here, the world seemed to hold its breath, as if allowing a sacred space for secrets to be whispered and hearts to find solace.

Waiting there was Matteo. He stood by the fountain, his silhouette framed by the moonlight, giving him an almost ethereal glow. The sight of him stirred something deep within Giovanni, a profound mix of longing, relief, and a love so profound it threatened to consume him. The weight of the Morosini name, the whispered rumours, the looming responsibilities - all momentarily faded into oblivion, replaced by the magnetic pull of the man before him.

Their reunion, as always was one of passion and warmth. In that embrace, the world outside ceased to exist. All that mattered was the feel of Matteo's arms around him, the warmth of their bodies pressed close, and the familiar scent that always seemed to transport Giovanni to a world where love knew no bounds.

As they pulled apart, Matteo traced the lines of Giovanni's face, his fingers lingering on the slightly furrowed brow, an indicator of the thoughts that often clouded the Morosini heir's mind. "You seem distant tonight," Matteo murmured, concern evident in his gaze.

Giovanni sighed, the weight of his reality rushing back. It was here, in this secluded paradise, he felt a semblance of peace. And with Matteo by his side, he felt read to face the challenges that lay ahead. With a deep exhale, he began, "Matteo, the world sees the Morosini crest, the grandeur, and the legacy. They witness the grand balls, the influence, and the wealth. But they don't see the shackles, the chains of expectation, and the labyrinth of responsibilities that come intertwined with the name."

Matteo, sensing the depth of emotion Giovanni was diving into, reached out and intertwined their fingers. The gesture, simple yet profound, served as an anchor, grounding Giovanni in the present moment.

"Our family's recent ascendancy, it's like we're on a tightrope," Giovanni continued, his voice laden with emotion, "One misstep, one slip of the tongue, and it could all come crumbling down. I'm expected to be the pillar, the stalwart protector of our legacy, but at times, I feel like a puppet, my strings tugged and pulled in a million directions."

Matteo took a moment to process Giovanni's words. The fountain's gentle lullaby and the night's serenade enveloped them, offering a brief interlude of silence. "Gio," Matteo began, using the nickname reserved only for their most intimate moments, "I can't fathom the golden bars of the cage you're trapped within, but know this: wealth and stature, they are transient. They ebb ad flow like the tides. What remains constant is your hear, your essence, and your soul."

Giovanni looked into Matteo's eyes, those deep pools reflecting sincerity and a depth of understanding that was beyond his years. "It's not just the expectations," Giovanni whispered, his voice barely audible, "It's the isolation. Surrounded by a sea of faces, yet feeling profoundly alone. Every smile, every gesture analysed. Every decision dissected."

Matteo, drawing Giovanni closer, replied, "And that's

why places like this, moments like these, they matter. Here, you are not Giovanni Morosini, the heir to an empire. You are just Giovanni, a man with dreams, fears, and a heart that knows love."

For a moment, the weight that Giovanni bore seemed to lighten. In the sanctuary of the courtyard and in the embrace of his love, he found a fleeting sense of freedom. The two souls, so different in their worlds yet bound by a love that transcended societal norms, sat there, united in their shared moment of vulnerability and understanding.

Time, it seemed, stood still. The city's distant hum, the courtyard's eternal charm, and two hearts conversing in silent understanding created an ambiance of raw, unfiltered emotion. And in that profound silence, amidst the poetic dance of moonlight and shadow, their bond deepened, finding strength in shared trials and dreams of a world unshackled from expectations.

The gentle chirping of crickets and the soft whispers of the night breeze framed their tranquil haven, cradling the two souls in nature's embrace. As the moments ebbed, Matteo, gathering a breath laden with memories, began to paint a vivid tableau of his world - a world that stood in stark contrast to the opulence of the Morosini legacy.

"In our small abode," he began, the trace of a wistful smile playing on his lips, "we don't have gilded walls or chandeliers that scatter prisms of light. But, oh, how the morning sun pours in through our modest windows, casting a warm golden hue over the worn wooden floor. It's as if each day, the universe bestows its own rich tapestry of sunlight upon us."

Giovanni, rapt in attention, imagined the sight. The description, so simple yet so poignant, tugged at his heartstrings. He realised that luxury wasn't always about grandeur; sometimes, it was found in the smallest details, in moments of serenity carved from the chaos of life.

Matteo's voice, tinged with nostalgia, continued, "Papa, he's a craftsman, holding clay into masterpieces. To the world, they are mere pots and vases, but to him, each is a story, an emotion, a fragment of his soul. Mama often jokes that he speaks more to his clay than he does to her," Matteo chuckled, the sound echoing like a melodious note in the stillness.

"And then there's Mia, my baby sister," his voice softened, "every evening, she dances. Not in grand ballrooms, but in our tiny courtyard, beneath the embrace of the twilight sky. Her laughter, her twirls, they're a testament to the simply joys life offers."

Drawing a deep breath, Matteo's gaze met Giovanni's. "But it's not just mirth and merriment, Gio. Each day is a battle, a struggle. To find enough work, to ensure there's food on our table. The weight of their aspirations for me, their hopes that I'd break free from this cycle, it's a burden I carry every waking moment."

Giovanni, absorbing the depth of Matteo's words, whispered, "Your world, it's filled with its own set of chains, yet it resonates with authenticity, with genuine emotion."

Matteo nodded, "Indeed. Our worlds, though galaxies apart, converge in this: the relentless pursuit of dreams, the weight of expectations, and the pressures of legacy. For Papa wishes for me to elevate our family's status, to venture beyond our modest means, to ensure Mia has the future he could never give her."

A gentle silence settled between them. Two souls, born into contrasting tapestries of life, yet bound by shared tribulations. The vast piazza, with its ancient stones and whispered secrets, bore testament to their bond - a connection that transcended the divides of society, bridging the chasm between privilege and simplicity.

Matteo, breaking the silence, mused, "Perhaps it's these shared burdens, these parallel struggles, that have entwined our fates, drawing us into this dance of love and longing."

Giovanni, moved by the profundity of the moment, responded, "In the vast mosaic of existence, amidst countless souls, our paths crossed, not by mere chance, but by a design far greater than we can fathom."

Their quiet breathing, in rhythm with the gentle ebb and flow of the night, created a cocoon of peace. The world beyond - it's expectations, judgements, and bindings - seemed distant. It was a transient, sacred bubble, where time held its breath and the universe conspired to protect their shared solitude.

Yet, the silence, thick with unsaid emotions, was interrupted when Matteo's fingers brushed against the edge of a sketched image of a sapphire in Giovanni's leather-bound notebook. His hazel eyes, reflecting the curiosity's glow, lifted to meet Giovanni's.

"Ah, the famed sapphire," he began, the shadows of overheard whispers darkening his voice, "the streets, they talk, Giovanni. They talk of a gem that brought fortune to the Morosinis."

Giovanni, realising that evading the topic would only fan the flames of curiosity, took a deep breath, choosing his words carefully, "The sapphire, I don't believe that it's just a gem, Matteo. It's history, legacy, it's a responsibility we never asked for."

The light from a hanging lantern danced across Giovanni's face, deepening the valleys of his furrowed brow and accentuating the earnestness in his eyes. "Since its arrival, our estate is aflutter, like a heart unsure of its own beat. The jewel, though magnificent, carries with it tales and truths. Tales of our ancestors, and truths of the power it wields."

He paused, allowing the weight of his words to settle. "With the sapphire came prestige, respect, an elevated status within the Venetian echelons. Yet, with those came envy, scrutiny, whispers that look to pierce our walls and get a glimpse of our newfound legacy."

Matteo, absorbing the gravity, pondered aloud, "But surely, a gem, no matter how enchanting, can't influence the course of life?"

Giovanni, looking deep into Matteo's eyes, whispered, "Perhaps, or perhaps it's the belief in its power that's the true catalyst. When a narrative is whispered enough, it starts to wear the cloak of truth. The sapphire might just be a beautiful relic from the past, or it might be a beacon drawing towards us energies we don't yet comprehend."

A serene silence settled between them. The sapphire, a symbol of the Morosini's ascent, was also a reminder of the delicate balance between privilege and vulnerability.

Matteo, placing a gentle hand on Giovanni's, said,

"Whether myth or reality, treasure or trial, remember, Gio, that the true strength of your family's legacy doesn't like in gems or gold. It's in the love you share, the bond that ties you together."

Giovanni nodded, the weight of the world slightly alleviated by the understanding shared in that intimate courtyard. The night, a silent witness to their confidences, continued its eternal dance, wrapping them in a veil of tranquility and ephemeral solace.

Amidst the orchestration of crickets and the gentle rustling of leaves, Matteo ventured, his voice hesitant yet filled with a dreamy quality, "Have you ever thought, Gio, of a place… a world, perhaps, where our souls could run free? Without the restraints of names and titles, without the judgments that echo in hallowed halls?"

Giovanni looked at him, eyes deep as the ocean, shimmering with unshed tears of hopes and dreams. "Every day, every moment, every stolen glance," he whispered. "A world where our love isn't an act of defiance but just a simple, beautiful truth."

They sat side by side, their fingers entwined, painting visions of this utopia in the canvas of their minds. Visions of a small cottage nestled amidst rolling hills, where mornings began with the sound of chirping birds and evenings were bathed in the golden hues of twilight. A world where their love story wasn't written in stolen moments but stretched endlessly, like the horizon that knows no end.

Yet, in the delicate fabric of this dream, a thread of dread weaved its presence. The reality of their world, the world outside this sacred sanctuary, posed threats too tangible to ignore. And it was Giovanni, with the Morosini name hanging heavily around his neck, who felt its weight the most.

"You know," he began, his voice a mere tremor, betraying the tempest of emotions within, "the streets, they talk. Not just of sapphires and legacy, but of whispers, secrets… secrets like ours."

Matteo's face paled, but his grip on Giovanni's hand tightened. "Gio, we knew the risks, the stakes of our shared moments. But love, it's worth it, isn't it?"

Giovanni smiled, a smile that spoke of love and pain in equal measure. "Always worth it. But the Morosini blood, it's both a privilege and a curse. If word gets out, if our secret becomes a spectacle for the Venetian gossipmongers, it won't just be my name at stake. They could harm you, try to tarnish your family, just to get back at mine."

Matteo leaned in, his forehead resting against Giovanni's. "Then let's be careful, even more than before. We've danced on the precipice of society's norms; we've tasted the thrill and the fear it brings. A few more stolen moments, a few more secrets kept, until perhaps… perhaps the world is ready for our tale."

Giovanni kissed Matteo's forehead, sealing their pact of hope and caution. "I dream of that day," he murmured, "when our love isn't a forbidden sonnet but an anthem sung out loud.

Entwined in their bond, the lovers found solace amid the chaos of their own emotions. In each other's arms, they sought refuge from the world that threatened to tear them apart. Matteo's fingers traced patterns on Giovanni's palm each line and curve representing dreams yet to be realised and challenges still to face. "Gio," he whispered, a note of hope dancing in his eyes, "Have you ever considered, perhaps… leaving it all behind?"

Giovanni, lost in the warmth of Matteo's touch, took a moment to respond. "Leave Venice?" he murmured, the very thought a storm of trepidation and longing. "Run away from everything we've ever known?"

Matteo nodded slowly. "Not forever, but maybe just long enough for us to breath, to live without looking over our shoulders. A place outside the city's grasp, away from prying eyes and whispered judgments. Somewhere we could just be… us."

Giovanni let the words wash over him, the idea like a siren's call - seductive yet filled with unknown dangers. "It's a dream," he admitted, "One I've entertained more often than I care to admit. But to leave behind the Morosini name, the responsibilities…"

Matteo cut him off gently, pressing a finger to Giovanni's lips. "I'm not saying forever, just moments, days even, stolen from the grand tapestry of life. Time that belongs only to us."

In the comforting hush of the night, Giovanni let himself imagine such a world. A secluded cottage nestled amidst verdant meadows, kissed by the golden sun and serenaded by chirping birds. A haven untouched by the burdens of legacy and societal expectations.

Matteo's eyes sparkled with excitement. "I've heard tales of old estates, abandoned and forgotten, just a few hours' journey from here. They could be our secret refuge, a place where our love story finds its true canvas."

Giovanni leaned in, captivated by the vision Matteo painted. "An escape," he breathed, the weight of the world momentarily lifted from his shoulders. "But we must be cautious. If even a whisper of our sanctuary reached the wrong ears…"

"We'll be discreet," Matteo assured, his fingers entwining with Giovanni's. "It'll be our little world, hidden in plain sight."

As the first tendrils of dawn started weaving their golden tapestry across the horizon, a gentle yet insistent reminder of time's relentless march, the lovers found themselves consumed by an emotion greater than the sum of their fears and hopes. Giovanni and Matteo, in the fleeting embrace of twilight, began to lay the foundations for their shared dreams, detailing every nuance. For them, the envisioned sanctuary was not just a physical retreat but a soulful testimony to love that boldly defied the world's constraints.

"Before we are swallowed by the approaching day," Matteo began, hesitating just a moment before reaching into the folds of his simple robe. From it, he produced a small pendant, hand-carved with an intricate design that seemed to dance and shimmer in the dim light.

Giovanni's eyes widened as he took in the details of the pendant, a masterful portrayal of two figures, their forms intertwined, reaching out towards a single star. "Matteo," he whispered, his voice thick with emotion, "this is…"

"Us," Matteo finished for him, his eyes reflecting the intensity of the moment. "I carved it during those nights when I longed for your presence. It's a symbol, Gio, of what we share, of promises spoken and unspoken, of dreams we've crafted and the journey ahead."

Giovanni, touched deeply, gently took the pendant, feeling its weight, both physical and symbolic. Holding it close to his chest, he said, "Every beat of my heart will now echo the essence of this gift, a constant reminder of our bond." The intricacies of the pendant seemed to capture the essence of their shared moments, the delicate balance of joy, sorrow, anticipation, and most importantly, love.

Matteo, his face illuminated by a radiant glow, moved closer, letting the distance between them vanish. Their hands met, fingers intertwining in a familiar dance, both finding strength and solace in the touch. "Promise me," Matteo whispered, his voice laced with a gentle urgency, "that no matter where our paths take us, no matter the challenges ahead, you'll hold onto this. Let it be our anchor."

Giovanni nodded, the weight of the promise settling on his shoulders. "Every sunrise and every sunset, every stolen moment and every dream, this pendant will be a part of it. I promise."

As the world around them began to stir awake, the lovers, ensconced in their shared bubble of timelessness, held onto each other. The embrace was both an affirmation and a farewell, the merging of two souls seeking to etch every sensation, every heartbeat into memory.

The silhouette they formed against the backdrop of a dawning sky was poignant and powerful. Two figures, united by a love that dared to challenge norms, stood as a testament to passions that burned bright, undiminished by society's judgment. The embrace lingered, either willing to be the first to let go, but time, ever the adversary, reminded them of the world beyond.

With a final, lingering touch and a promise of stolen moments to come, the two parted. The horizon, painted with hues of rose and gold, watched as they disappeared in opposite directions. And while the streets of the city would soon be bustling, for a brief moment, all that existed was the echo of a love so profound that it would forever remain etched in the annals of time.

Chapter 5

The grandeur of the Morosini Palazzo on this particular evening was nothing short of breathtaking. The grand facade, a testament to the affluence and artistry of its owners, shimmered brilliantly, bathed in the golden glow of countless lanterns and torches. Each flickering flame was reflected a hundredfold in the eyes of the city's elite who approached its opulent gates, their countenances painted with an admixture of anticipation and sheer awe.

From its towering spires to its expansive courtyards, the palazzo was a veritable haven of lights, each meticulously placed to cast ethereal shadows and highlight the stunning architectural marvels contained within. Enormous draperies of silks and velvets in deep burgundies, emerald greens, and midnight blues hung from the balconies, dancing gracefully in the evening breeze, echoing the movements of the guests below.

The intoxicating aroma of blooming jasmine, paired with the exotic scents of burning incense, pervaded the atmosphere, creating a tapestry of olfactory delight. As guests traversed the sprawling gardens, they were greeted by the gentle play of water fountains, their cascades shimmering under the moonlight, reminiscent of liquid silver. Majestic peacocks roamed the grounds, their plumes a spectacular display of iridescence, each feather catching the ambient light and refracting it in a myriad of colours.

In the heart of this palatial expanse, the grand ballroom

opened its arms to the creme de la creme of society. A colossal chandelier, resplendent with thousands of crystals, hung from the vaulted ceiling, cascading a spectrum of lights upon the polished marble floors below. Its illumination was so luminous that the room below seemed to sway, ebb, and flow in its luminescent embrace.

The dulcet tones of a string quartet resonated through the grandeur, the musicians stationed upon a dais, their fingers dancing upon instrument strings with a masterful precision that was both heartwarming and evocative. Each note, rising a falling with impeccable timing, weaved tales of romance, valour, and poignant farewells, moving the very souls of those who paused to listen. The music lent an atmosphere of elegance and splendour, making hearts soar and spirits waltz. The very air seemed to thrum with the melodies, vibrating with the age-old rhythms of passion, sorrow, and unbridled joy.

The ballroom floor itself was a whirl of colours. Ladies in sumptuous gowns, their fabrics sourced from the far reaches of the Orient and beyond, glided gracefully, their every move a testament to the hours of preparation that had preceded this evening. Their parents, dapper in tailored suits and crisply ironed cravats, led them in dances that spoke of traditions and etiquettes, of courtships and alliances.

Off to the side, tables laden with gastronomic delights awaited the guests. There were platters of roasted game, their aromas tantalising, complemented by a selection of the finest wines sourced from the sun-kissed vineyards of Tuscany. Exquisite pastries, each a miniature artwork, beckoned the guests, promising a burst of flavours with every bite.

Outside the ballroom, in the quieter alcoves of the palazzo, the more introspective guests found solace. Here, away from the dazzling lights and the vivacity of the dance floor, they could gaze upon the vast skies, their thoughts lost among the constellations. The gardens, meticulously manicured and dotted with statues of alabaster and bronze, offered serene pathways where one could stroll and lose oneself in reverie.

It was, by every measure, an evening that would be etched into the annals of the city's history. A night where the Morosini family, with every flickering lantern, every note of music, and every laughter-filled conversation, solidified their place among the elite, note just as prosperous merchants but as patrons of the arts, culture and the very essence of refined civilisation.

Amidst the resplendence of the ballroom, where the cascade of lights played with shadows and where the music intertwined with the beating hearts of its audience, the dance floor became a theatre. On this grand stage, narratives unfolded, tales of alliances, rivalries, past lovers, and new passions. Yet, of all these stories, one would rise to captivate the attention of all present.

Liliana, the prized jewel of the Morosini household, appeared nothing less than ethereal. Cloaked in a gown that seemed to borrow its hues from the very night sky, she was an embodiment of celestial elegance. The dress flowed in layers of deep indigo, punctuated with brilliant sequinned constellations. It shimmered and danced, much like the stars overhead, making her seem as if she'd emerged from a painter's dream, where midnight and magic merged. Her raven-black tresses were adorned with silver hairpins that twinkled with each subtle movement, mirroring the twinkling stars in the vast firmament.

Antonio Bellini, on the other hand, presented a striking contrast yet was no less captivating. Dressed in a sharp, tailored suit of charcoal grey, he wore a crisply folded pocket square and an intricate brooch, both in shades that complemented Liliana's gown. His dark hair was pulled back, emphasising his sharp jawline and intense, penetrating eyes. Those eyes, usually reserved for negotiations and trade deliberations, tonight bore an uncharacteristic softness, a hint of vulnerability.

The vastness of the ballroom, with its opulent chandeliers and the flurry of dancers, could often drown individuals in its grand tapestry. Yet, when Liliana's cerulean eyes met the deep brown of Antonio's from across the room, everything else seemed to blur. It was as though a silent sonnet of yearning and admiration passed between them, unspoken but deeply felt.

The room, already abuzz with chatter and music, felt the electric charge of this moment. Whispers swirled around, curious and anticipatory. The union of two such individuals, both in status and attraction, was an irresistible spectacle.

When Antonio approached, extending a hand in invitation, Liliana's heart skipped a beat, but her poise remained unbroken. As their fingers intertwined, and they took their position, the world around them receded. The quartet's melodies seemed to find a new fervour, a deeper resonance, as if they too recognised the significance of this union.

The two danced with a grace that was enchanting. The chemistry between them was palpable, each step, each twirl articulating emotions words could never convey. The very air around them seemed to throb, heavy with silent exchanges and stolen glances. Their movements were in perfect harmony, echoing the rhythm of two hearts that, while meeting for the first time on such an intimate platform, seemed to have known each other for eons.

As they glided across the floor, the onlookers could sense the simmering tension of unsaid feelings. Every touch, every look hinted at a story waiting to be written, a blossoming relationship that promised tales of passion, challenges, and unwavering devotion.

When the music reached its crescendo, Antonio spun Liliana in an intricate twirl, her gown flaring, making her seem like a nebula, a celestial entity that had descended onto the ballroom. As the last note faded, and their dance concluded, the room erupted in applause, not just for the mesmerising performance, but also in acknowledgement of the bond that had unmistakable formed.

As they parted, a gentle squeeze of hands, a lingering look, spoke of promises and dreams. Their dance may have ended, but it was evident to all present that the story of Liliana Morosini and Antonio Bellini had only just begun. Their union, whether forged by fate or serendipity, became the talk of the evening, a beacon of romance in an event that celebrated opulence and grandeur.

****

The grand ballroom, awash with the golden glow of candlelight and filled with the lilting harmonies of the string quartet, was a scene of splendour. Yet, amidst this resplendence, Leonora was a vision to behold. The grand matriarch exuded an air of regality, every inch the poised hostess revealing in her family's ascendancy.

Leonora was dressed in a flowing gown of rich emerald green, a hue reminiscent of the deepest forests, contrasting beautifully against her silver-streaked ebony hair, which was elegantly pinned up. Each fold and drape of her dress whispered tales of opulence, and the intricate golden embroidery hinted at a blend of tradition and wealth. However, it wasn't just her attire that captured the attention; it was the magnificent sapphire heirloom which rested majestically around her neck. The sapphire, set in a delicate lattice of silver, caught every beam of candlelight, reflecting a myriad of azure hues, each shade telling tales of history, power, and allure.

Leonora, with a keen sense of the moment, ensured that the sapphire was not just a piece of jewellery; it was a statement. As she moved gracefully through the room, the pendant would sway ever so slightly, ensuring that it caught the light - and, inevitable, many an eye. Each glance directed towards it, whether filled with admiration, envy, or sheer wonder, added to the narrative of the Morosini's rise.

The ballroom was filled with a veritable who's who of the city's elite. Nobles, merchants, artists, and thinkers - they were all present, their voices forming a symphony of laughter, chatter, and clinking glasses. But Leonora, in her role as the evening's hostess, ensured she missed none. She navigated the room with an enviable ease, her steps measured and her demeanour warm yet authoritative.

"Ah, Contessa Bianchi," Leonora greeted, her voice carrying just the right mix of warmth and formality, "It brings me immense joy to see you grace our humble abode this evening."

The Contessa, a formidable figure in her own right, responded with a nod, her eyes inadvertently drawn to the sapphire. "Your home is magnificent, Signora Morosini. And that pendant, it's truly one of a kind."

Leonora, seizing the opportunity, replied, "Thank you, dear Contessa. It is an heirloom that has recently come into our possession. They say it carries with it stories from epochs gone by."

The subtle emphases was not lost on those listening. The sapphire wasn't merely a symbol of wealth; it was an embodiment of the Morosini family's rising status, their place amongst the city's luminaries.

Throughout the evening, similar exchanges unfolded. Each interaction, every compliment directed towards the sapphire, was a brick in the edifice of the Morosini's reputation. Leonora's grace, combined with her shrewdness, ensured that the narrative of the evening was not just about a grand ball, but also about a family's metric ascent.

However, it wasn't just about pomp and show. There were genuine moments of warmth too. When she approached old friends, her eyes would light up, her laughter more heartfelt. In these moments, the weight of the sapphire seemed to lessen, replaced by the lightness of genuine human connection.

Yet, as the evening wore on, it was clear that Leonora's display was strategic. The sapphire, with its mesmerising allure, was more than just a gemstone; it was a tool, a beacon signalling the Morosini's prominence.

As she finally paused, taking a moment to survey the grand ballroom, its dancing guests, the sparkling crystal, and the resounding melodies, a sense of satisfaction washed over her. In the heart of this magnificent spectacle, Leonora, with the sapphire heirloom as her aid, had successfully showcased her family's stature.

****

Amid the swirling vortex of the grand ball, Giovanni stood like an island of contemplation in a sea of revelry. As attendees danced, gossiped, and revealed, Giovanni's gaze was a sweeping beacon, subtly observing the ballroom's intricacies. To the casual observer, he seemed lost in pleasantries, engaging in dialogues with guests. However, each exchange, every handshake and nod, was a strategic maneuver in Giovanni's internal chess game. He was alert to every word spoken, every laugh shared, discerning alliances, potential threats, and the myriad undercurrents that churned beneath the surface of this gathering.

His sharp eyes, those discerning orbs that missed no detail, however minute, eventually settled upon a particular dance. Liliana, his beloved sister, radiant and resplendent in her celestial gown, was dancing with Antonio Bellini, the merchant whose reputation was as vast as his wealth. The dance was a juxtaposition of grace and fervour, a ballet of stolen glances and hands delicately held. It was evident to Giovanni, as he watched them sway to the rhythm, that there was genuine affection brewing between the two.

Giovanni noted the way Antonio's fingers lightly brushed against Liliana's, the way his gaze lingered just a second too long on her face, absorbing every feature, every nuance of her expression. The soft include of his head as he listener intently to her whispered words, the shadow of a smile that danced on his lips when she laughed - it all screamed of an affection that was pure and untainted. It warmed Giovanni's heart to see his sister, the one he had watched over since childhood, find such genuine connection.

Interrupting his observations, a fellow noble engaged Giovanni in conversation. But even as he discussed trade routes and recent political shifts, part of him remained anchored to that dance. Giovanni's senses were attuned to the nuances - the arch of Liliana's brow when Antonio whispered something in her ear, the slight tilt of Antonio's head when his gaze once again wandered to the sapphire.

As the song reached its crescendo and the couple finished their dance to applause, Giovanni took a mental note. There were layers to this evening, a multitude of stories being written in every corner of the ballroom. But the narrative of Liliana and Antonio, was one that required his careful vigilance.

****

In a place where splendour and spectacle reigned

supreme, it took a rare occurrence to punctuate the continued merriment and opulence. And so it was that amidst the glitz and laughter, a sudden profound stillness settled over the ballroom of the Morosini Palazzo.

The grand archways, illuminated by golden lanterns and festooned with silver draperies, cast a luminous frame around an enigmatic figure: Cecelia. Her entrance was like that of an otherworldly apparition, and the very atmosphere seemed to bend in her presence. Garbed in a somber dress of deeper midnight, embroidered with muted silver thread that mirrored the soft light of the stars, Cecelia moved with a graceful, haunting magnetism. The gown glowed around her like dark water, pooling in inky tides at her feet.

Though she was an invited guest, none had truly expected Cecelia to grace the event with her presence. Known for her reclusive nature, she was a tapestry of legends, a living enigma intertwined with tales of foresight, wisdom, and most pertinently, her association with the Morosini family heirloom.

As she moved, the ballroom's occupants instinctively parted, creating an open path for her. A symphony of whispers crescendoed around her, echoing her name and legacy. "Cecelia Adriana," they murmured, their voices a mix of reverence, curiosity, and apprehension. "The one who gifted the sapphire to the Morosinis."

Eyes, gleaming with intrigue and speculation, followed her every move. Some recalled tales of her mysterious origins, her fabled insights into realms beyond the tangible. Others exchanged whispers of the fateful day she had bestowed the now-infamous sapphire upon the Morosini family, intertwining their destinies forever.

Cecelia, with a grace untouched by the weight of years, carried herself with a silent majesty. Her raven-black hair cascaded down her back, intertwining with the ebony fabric of her dress. The only adornment she bore was a simple ruby pendant resting around her neck, glowing softly with an inner luminescence.

Though the weight of countless gazes pressed upon her, she seemed undisturbed, her countenance a serene reflection of moonlit waters. Yet, her eyes, dark orbs that seemed to have gazed upon the vast tapestry of time itself, bore a solemn intensity. They took in the grandeur, the dancing couples, the shimmering gowns, and the glint of the sapphire, worn so proudly be Leonora.

A few daring souls, driven by a mix of alcohol and curiosity, approached her, extending greetings or trying to engage her in light conversation. Cecelia, always courteous, responded with soft-spoken words, her voice a melodic whisper that seemed to carry the weight of ancient secrets.

As she moved through the hall, the atmosphere began to shift. The initial hush, born of surprise, began to transform into a palpable tension. Cecelia's presence, like a stone cast into still waters, created ripples that touched every corner of the ballroom.

But for all the grandeur and the whispered conversations she ignited, Cecelia's focus was singular. Her journey through the ballroom, though seemingly meandering, was purposeful. Each step, each graceful turn, drew her closer to the heart of the Morosini legacy and the sapphire that pulsed with an enigmatic energy. For now, however, she remained an observer, a shadowy presence wearing through the golden tapestry of the ball.

****

As hours passed, the intoxicating blend of wine and elation made the world around blur into an enchanting haze. It was during such a moment, when the revelry had returned to its peak, and the string quartet drew a lingering note to signal a lull, that Cecelia made her move.

The room, which returned to its canvas of constant motion, suddenly froze as Cecelia stepped forward. Every eye was drawn to her, the weight of her presence undeniable.

With a grace that belied the urgency in her eyes, Cecelia approached the gathering. Her steps echoed softly, each one resounding like the heartbeat of the room. The whispers and laughter that had previously filled the space faded once more, replaced by a breathless anticipation.

Drawing herself to her full, regal height, she addressed the room, but her words, laden with gravitas, were meant for Leonora. “Madam Morosini,” Cecelia began, her voice a hauntingly beautiful melody that seemed to weave through the air, “The gem you wear so proudly, the sapphire that graces your neck, is not merely an ornament. It is a beacon, a harbinger, holding powers that reach beyond our comprehension.”

The room remained ensnared in a hush, the gravity of Cecelia’s words hanging heavy. Faces that had been flushed with wine and laughter now turned pale, eyes widening in a mix of fear and fascination.

Leonora, ever the proud matriarch, met Cecelia's gaze, her chin lifted defiantly. The sapphire, which had been the crowning glory of her ensemble, now seemed to pulse ominously in the candlelight. Its facets captured the room's myriad colours, reflecting them back in an otherworldly dance. "You were gracious enough to gift it to us," Leonora replied, her voice dripping with feigned sweetness, "Should we not wear it with the pride it deserves?"

Cecelia's eyes, deep pools that held ageless wisdom, bore into Leonora's. "Pride, dear Leonora, can often blind us to truths that stand before our very eyes. The sapphire's allure is undeniable, but so are its consequences. It is a key, a gateway, and in the wrong hands, a weapon."

Murmurs rippled through the room, guests exchanging unease glances, the earlier merriment now a distant memory. Even the musicians, their bows hovering above their instruments, seemed hesitant to break the thick tension.

Leonora, visibly unsettled yet unwilling to show weakness, let out a soft chuckle. "Madam Cecelia," she began with an air of condescension, "While your tales are entertaining, this is neither the time nor place for such fantastical warnings. We are here to celebrate, not to be regaled with fairytales."

Cecelia, undeterred by Leonora's dismissive tone, spoke with a finality that sent chills down many a spine. "The sapphire's essence is intertwined with the very fabric of our world. Beware its call, for its song, while seductive, can also be a dirge. Heed my words, or the very foundations of the Morosini legacy may crumble."

The echo of Cecelia's warning lingered in the vast expanse of the ballroom, casting a momentary pall over the night's festivities. The flickering candles, which previously exuded warmth, now seemed to cast shadows that danced with a frenetic energy, mirroring the unease that had enveloped the gathering.

Leonora, however, stood resolute, the sapphire pendant upon her décolletage catching the light in defiant glimmers. The ever-astute matriarch, she understood the weight of the moment and recognised the need to reclaim control over the evening.

Her laughter, rich and melodic, cut through the stifling silence. "Dear Cecelia," she began, her voice imbued with a blend of pity and mockery, "Time has a cruel way of clouding our minds, does it not? While we cherish your past gifts and your association with our esteemed family, it seems the weight of years has brought with it some… fanciful imaginings."

Around the room, guests, exchanged uncertain glances, the atmosphere thick with tension. Some looked sympathetically at Cecelia, while others, eager to stay in the good graces of their hostess, wore tight-lipped smiles, nodding in agreement with Leonora.

The raging mystic, however, stood firm, her posture defiant. Her eyes deep wells of ancient knowledge, met Leonora's in a silent clash of wills. But before she could retort, Leonora continued, the silk of her voice masking the steel beneath. "Perhaps the excitement of the evening has been too much for you. It might be best, dear Cecelia, if you retired and sought some rest. Age, after all, requires its due."

A ripple of hushed whispers flowed through the crowd, the underlying note of scandal adding a piquant flavour to the evening's drama. The Morosini's ball had certainly become an event that would be discussed in hushed tones for weeks to come.

Refusing to be so easily dismissed, Cecelia's voice rang out, clear and resonant. "My age has gifted me with clarity, not confusion. I stand by my words, and while they may seem unsettling, they come from a place of genuine concern."

Leonora, sensing the mounting tension and eager to prevent any further disruptions, made a subtle motion with her hand. Almost immediately, two burly guards, dressed in the livery of the Morosini household, emerged from the periphery. Their imposing presence signalled an unspoken command: the time had come for Cecelia to depart.

"Madam," one of the guards intoned respectfully, extending an arm towards the exit, "please accompany us."

Cecelia, though visibly pained by the abrupt end to her entreaty, maintained her dignity. With a final, lingering look at Leonora and the glitter sapphire, she allowed the guards to escort her away, but not before declaring, "The truth, no matter how fervently denied, remains steadfast. Be wary of the path you tread, Leonora Morosini."

The room remained in stunned silence for a heartbeat longer, the gravity of the confrontation weight heavily upon every heart and mind present. Leonora, however, was quick to redirect the evening's narrative. With a flourish, she beckoned to the musicians, her voice light and jovial, "Let the music play on! We shall not let fleeting distractions dampen our spirits."

As the strings resumed their melodious enchantment and the night's revelries continued, an undercurrent of whispers persisted. But for most, the allure of the dance, the wine, and the merriment soon overshadowed the somber interruption, leaving the dire warning of an old mystic to fade into the night's memories. Yet, for a few, Cecelia's words would remain, a haunting refrain in the grand ball at the Morosini Palazzo.

****

As the ball's melodies ebbed and flowed, so did the current of whispers, rippling with intrigue, speculation, and conjecture. The confrontation between Leonora and Cecelia was like a stone cast into a placid lake, its ripples touching even the most distant shores of the room. The Morosini Palazzo had always been a nexus of Venetian society's events, but tonight, it became the very crucible of its most scintillating tales.

Clusters of guests huddled in corners, their masks barely concealing the spark of curiosity in their eyes. The sapphire, once the beacon of opulence and the Morosini family's resurgence, now shimmered with an aura of mystery and foreboding.

"I always suspected there was more to that jewel," murmured a dowager to her companion, her fan expertly masking her words from any eavesdroppers.

A young debutante whispered excitedly to her friend, "Can you imagine? A cursed gem in our midst! It's like one of those romantic tales of yore."

Amidst these fervent exchanges, there were also those who scoffed at the very notion, their skepticism pronounced in their dismissive tones. "Old Cecelia always had a penchant for theatrics," remarked a baron, sipping his wine nonchalantly. "Nothing more than the ramblings of age."

However, among the cacophony of whispers and half-truths, one figure remained particularly attuned, his intrigue manifesting not in gossipy asides but in measured, calculated conversation. Antonio Bellini had sensed an opportunity.

Using his natural charm and the art of conversation, he deftly navigated from one cluster of guests to the next, probing, inquiring, always listening. His questions seemed casual, even innocuous, but there was purpose in each word. "It's indeed a marvellous gem," he would remark, allowing his gaze to drift to Leonora's neck. "Do you know much of its origin?"

A nobleman, eager to flaunt his knowledge, responded, "Ah, it's said to have come from the East, from lands where magic still lingers in the air. But curses? Pat! Just tales to titillate the bored and the gullible."

Another guest, a lady with a penchant for collecting exotic artefacts, leaned in, her voice dropping to a conspiratorial whisper. "I've heard tales of such gems, bound with ancient powers. But whether they hold true power or simply the allure of legend, who can truly say?"

****

Liliana felt herself increasingly ensnared in a net of complexities that evening. Between the melodious strains of the quartet and the flicker of candlelight, a storm raged within her heart.

Slipping away from the gilded hall, she found herself drawn to the palazzo's private gardens, a sanctuary she had always sought in times of disquiet. The heady aroma of blooming roses and night-blooming jasmine enveloped her as she stepped onto the cobblestone path. Here, the night was a living tapestry of silvery moonlight, shimmering starlight, and the soft sighs of the breeze.

The confrontation between her mother and Cecelia weighed heavily upon her. The ominous warning, her mother's dismissive response, and the undercurrents of tension that flowed through the ballroom were all overwhelming. But beyond that, there was Antonio. The magnetic pull she felt towards him was undeniable.

As she wandered through the garden, the gentle murmur of the fountain and the soft glow of lanterns casting dappled light up on the flowers provided a soothing backdrop to her tumultuous thoughts. The sapphire, with its deep blue depths and mysterious allure, was more than just a gemstone; it was a legacy, an emblem of the family's resurgence, but with Cecelia's cryptic warnings it seemed to be more like a heavy chain around her mother's neck, its weight a constant reminder of responsibilities and potential threats.

Her thoughts turned to Antonio, and the dance they had shared earlier that evening. The connection between them was intense, a dance of souls as much as of bodies. She recalled the intensity in his eyes, the gentle grip of his hand, and the shared whispers that spoke of mutual attraction.

Liliana paused by a marble bench, canopied by a cascade of wisteria, its purple blooms gently swaying in the night breeze. She took a moment, drawing a deep breath, trying to find clarity amidst the whirlwind of emotions.

Above her, the vast expanse of the heavens glittered, a boundless sea of stars, each a beacon of hope in the dark tapestry of the night. Their ageless glow seemed to whisper ancient wisdom, urging her to trust her instincts and follow her heart. But in this world, the path forward was shrouded in uncertainty.

As she sat in silent contemplation, the soft rustle of the trees and the distant echoes of the ball's melodies seemed to blend, creating a lullaby for her troubled heart. With the starlit sky as her confidante, Liliana found herself at a precipice.

****

As the final strains of music began to fade and the illustrious guests of the Morosini ball made their way towards their awaiting carriages, the grand Palazzo that had witnessed so much revelry seemed to exhale, settling into the profound silence of post-celebration. Golden candlelight glinted across the opulent ballroom, creating fleeting shadows that danced in tandem with the residual echoes of laughter and murmured conversations.

Gathered in a more intimate drawing room, with its lavish tapestries and ornate chandeliers, the Morosini family stood, reflecting on the evening's myriad of events. The successful hosting of the grand ball would be spoken about for months, perhaps even years. Yet, interwoven with the pleasure of their success was the unsettling confrontation with Cecelia and her dire warning.

Leonora voiced her thoughts. "Despite unforeseen challenges, tonight has been a triumph. Our family's position in society has been firmly cemented." The sapphire's glint around her neck seemed to amplify her sentiments.

Liliana, lost in her thoughts and the night's conflicting emotions, silently contemplated the significance of Antonio's presence and Cecelia's words. Her heart was a battleground of affections and apprehensions.

As they continued to share their individual perspectives, Giovanni, with a deepened furrow of concern on his brow, drew the family close, lowering his voice as though fearful of being overheard by the walls themselves.

"In the midst of the celebrations," he began, a grim seriousness to his tone, "my private chambers were intruded upon." A collective gasp escaped the gathered family, the weight of the implications heavy in the room. "Upon my return," Giovanni continued, "though I found nothing amiss or missing, there was a singular emblem left behind on my desk."

He unveiled a small, intricate brooch, the likes of which he hadn't seen before. Crafted in dark metal, it bore no recognisable insignia of any Venetian house, but was simply the shape of a raven. Its unfamiliarity was deeply unnerving.

"Could this be a signature," mused Liliana, "a mark of

some rival faction or secret society?"

Leonora's eyes narrowed. "It's a clear message," she declared. "We are being watched, and tonight's events have not gone unnoticed."

As they pondered the implications of the emblem, a sudden chill seemed to cascade through the room. It was an inexplicable coldness, cutting through the warm embrace of the heart. Leonora instinctively clutched the sapphire necklace, its icy touch strangely colder than usual.

Before anyone could speak, a mournful wail pierced the silence, echoing hauntingly through the palazzo's now-deserted hallways. The sound was ethereal, otherworldly - a lament that seemed to resonate from both the distant past and an uncertain future.

The family, rooted to their spots, exchanged alarmed glances. Was the palazzo haunted? Or was this another warning, far more chilling than Cecelia's ominous words? The very walls of the palazzo seemed to resonate with the weight of unsaid tales and hidden histories.

The immediate aftermath of the haunting wail left an oppressive stillness in the palatial chamber. Each member of the Morosini family stood suspended in that weighty hush, their faces reflecting the interplay of disbelief, fear, and concern. They were a lineage accustomed to the predictability of their world, where every happening, every event, was governed by reason. Yet here, in the familiar embrace of their ancestral home, the inexplicable had left them momentarily adrift.

Leonora attempted to marshal her thoughts, her fingers subconsciously reaching for the pulsating sapphire that lay against her chest. The stone, with its deep blue depths, seemed to hold within it a swirling tempest, a reflection of the storm of emotions that threatened to engulf the family.

Giovanni, usually a figure of composure, took a deep, steadying breath. "We are confronted with circumstances that lie beyond the scope of our understanding," he began, his voice a blend of determination and gravitas. "Yet, we must not allow fear to govern our actions or dictate our decisions."

Liliana, her porcelain features illuminated by the soft candlelight, added, "We have always navigated our way through challenges with poise and discretion. And though this… phenomenon is unlike any we've encountered, our resolve remains unchanged."

It wasn't bravado that united them, but a deep-seated resilience. The Morosinis were not just a family of affluence but of influence, a legacy that was cultivated through generations of facing adversity head-on. The recent events - Cecelia's dire warning, the mysterious emblem, and now this ghostly lament - were threads of a larger tapestry that they were only just beginning to discern.

But as dawn's first light began to pierce the darkness outside, casting elongated shadows on the ornate walls of the Palazzo, the family drew strength from their collective resolve. Uncertainty might loom, but they would face it with the grace, intelligence, and discretion that had always defined their legacy.

In the heavy stillness that followed, the flicker of a candle's shadow danced unsettlingly against the windowpane, suggesting a presence unseen yet palpably felt, beckoning a dread they could not name.

Chapter 6

As the Venetian sun dipped low, casting its golden radiance upon cobblestones and water, Liliana and Antonio found themselves enveloped in its magic.

On a particularly serene evening, a gondola, piloted by a seasoned gondolier humming a nostalgic tune, became their vessel of exploration. As Antonio shared tales of faraway lands and adventures, Liliana listened, rapt, her eyes catching the play of sunset on the water. The delicate dance of light, the surreal stillness of the evening, and Antonio's animated stories converged into moments that seemed suspended in time.

But the city of water wasn't just about quiet canals. The echoing laughter of children playing by the streets, the aroma of freshly baked bread, the distant sound of church bells - all contributed to their shared experiences. On one sunlit afternoon, beneath the shade of an old oak, they sat surrounded by a spread the finest Italian delicacies. Their conversation flowed, meandering through hopes, dreams, and shared laughter, the world beyond momentarily forgotten.

Venetian operas, those grand spectacles of art and emotions, beckoned them too. In opulent halls, under the shimmering glow of grand chandeliers, they let the poignant melodies carry them away. With every high note, every dramatic pause, they leaned closer, the music forging an unspoken bond between them.

With the passage of days, Antonio's gestures grew in warmth and grandeur. Delicate bouquets adorned with the freshest roses and dahlias found their way to Liliana's chambers. Chocolates, smooth and delectable, accompanied hand-written notes that spoke of affection and longing. Among the plethora of gifts was a particularly striking locket, ornate and vintage, housing within it Antonio's miniature portrait, a silent promise of devotion.

Beyond just the alleys and palazzos, the city was also crafted by the myriad secluded spots it housed, pockets of serenity in a city pulsing with life and secrets. On an afternoon when the sun's golden hues kissed the earth and the air carried whispers of blooming flowers, Antonio led Liliana to one such hidden sanctuary.

Nestled away from the usual hum of city life, a quaint garden blossomed in secret. A halo of ivy-clad walls shielded it, with flowers draping themselves in cascades from ancient stone statues. The centre boasted a languid pool, its surface so still that it mirrored the world around it, interrupted only by the sporadic dance of water lilies.

They walked, hand in hand, the gravel crunching softly beneath their feet, punctuating the hushed conversations of nature. Antonio spoke of childhood escapades, of a time when responsibilities were unknown and every dawn heralded new adventures. He recounted tales of sailing across the Adriatic, of the nights when stars seemed within arm's reach and the sea whispered tales of old.

Liliana listened, her heart synchronising with his tales, sharing in return stories of her sheltered upbringing, of the walls of the Morosini palazzo which bore witness to her joys and sorrows. She narrated tales of her late father, of nights spent under the vast canvas of the night sky, stargazing and weaving stories about constellations. They shared dreams, fears, hopes, and vulnerabilities, two souls intertwining amidst a backdrop of unparalleled beauty.

In that garden, time seemed to bow to their will, stretching moments into infinity. Seated by the pool, they watched as the sun cast elongated shadows, turning the garden into a realm of contrasts, light battling the encroaching darkness. It was there that Antonio, with a hesitance uncharacteristic of him, reached out, tucking a stray whisper of hair behind Liliana's ear, his fingers lingering against the warmth of her skin.

Drawn into the depths of each other's gaze, the world faded into a mere murmur. It was a moment crystallised in time, two hearts converging, tethered by threads of affection and longing. Their foreheads met, the distance between them measured now by mere breaths, their souls resonating with the silent serenades of love.

As dusk approached and the garden was bathed in a soft twilight, Antonio and Liliana promised each other many more such rendezvous, cherishing the bond that was blossoming between them.

****

Tucked away from the prying eyes of a bustling city, Taverna dell'Ombra had long stood as the unofficial meeting ground for those entangled in the darker recesses of power and treachery. Its walls, which had seen countless secrets traded and devious plans hatched, absorbed the clandestine tales, sealing them away from the world outside.

Upon entering, Antonio felt the shift in the air - the thick atmosphere, laden with whispers of past conspiracies. The was a raw authenticity to this place. The scents of aged wood, burning tobacco, and spilt ale blended in an oddly comforting aroma, one that welcomed all, regardless of intent.

He glanced around, noting the patrons - a mix of rugged individuals lost in their drinks some sharing hushed conversations, others merely savouring the refuge the tavern offered from their mysterious pursuits. At the fathest corner, a dimply lit booth beckoned. There, a shadowed figure awaited, as still as the night itself, wrapped in a dark hooded cloak with a raven brooch.

Taking a deep breath, Antonio approached. The wooden floor beneath creaked softly with every step, announcing his presence. As he slid into the booth, the figure stirred, revealing just a hint of a chiseled, weather-beaten face. The eyes, however, shone with sharp intelligence, betraying a mind that missed nothing.

"You're late," the figure murmured, his voice a raspy whisper that barely traveled past their booth.

Antonio, not one to be easily intimidated, replied, "I had to ensure I wasn't followed."

The figure chuckled, "Always the careful one. Very well. What news do you bring?"

Taking a moment to gather his thoughts, Antonio began, "The heirloom. The legendary Sapphire of Morosini. It's closer than we think. Leonora, the matriarch, has it."

Leaning back, the figure absorbed this information, his gaze never leaving Antonio. "And you're sure of this?"

Antonio nodded, "Almost certain. But procuring it... that's a different matter. The palazzo's security is legendary. More than just guards and walls, there are whispered tales of enchanted protections."

The man smirked, revealing a hint of amusement. "Enchantments? Really, Antonio? You surprise me with such superstitious beliefs."

Antonio countered, "This isn't mere superstition. The Morosini line has always been intertwined with the arcane. The sapphire itself is said to be imbued with ancient magic. Underestimating its power could be our downfall."

There was a silence as the mysterious man contemplated this revelation. "So, the risks are even higher than anticipated. Yet, its potential yield, both in power and wealth, is unparalleled."

Feeling the weight of the moment, Antonio took a deep breath. "There's more. My relationship with Liliana grants me certain insights, privileges even. I've seen portions of the palazzo others can only dream of. But the deeper layers, where the sapphire likely rests, remain a mystery."

The figure, now genuinely intrigued, leaned in closer. "You speak of layers. What do you mean?"

Antonio hesitated, then decided to trust. "Hidden chambers, secret corridors. The palazzo is an architectural marvel, designed to protect its most prized possession."

The man raised an eyebrow, "So, we're not just dealing with guards and potential enchantments, but also a maze?"

"Yes," Antonio admitted.

The figure seemed to muse over this. "Very well. We'll need a plan, one that factors in all these challenges. A partnership seems inevitable."

Antonio nodded in agreement. "Together, we can achieve what neither can do alone."

The mysterious man offered a hand, "Then let's seal our fates."

As their hands clasped in agreement, the very foundations of the tavern seemed to shudder, as if sensing the gravity of the pact that was just forged.

The meeting's shadowy ambiance was further intensified as the figure reached inside his cloak, producing a delicately crafted vial. It shimmered with an eerie luminescence, the muted glow standing in stark contrast to the tavern's dull, ambient light. Even in the dim setting, the liquid inside appeared to be constantly shifting, a silence dance of shades between deepest indigo and translucent cerulean.

Seeing Antonio's gaze fixed on the vial, the man said, "This, my friend, is your key to the palazzo's inner sanctum. It has taken considerable resources and time to perfect this elixir. When released into the air, it will plunge every living being that breaths it into a profound slumber. Even the most vigilant of guards won't stand a chance."

Antonio took the vial cautiously, examining the entrancing liquid. "How does it work? Is it… lethal?"

The man shook his head. "No. It merely incapacitates, ensuring a deep, dreamless sleep. They'll awaken hours later with no recollection of events during their enforced rest. It's an art, you see, balancing potency with safety. We need the guards out of our way, not dead."

Drawing a thoughtful breath, Antonio queried, "And its range? How much ground will this cover?"

The figure leaned closer, his voice barely above a whisper, "Just a few drops can cast its spell on a small room. The entire vial is enough to subdue the guards of a sizeable portion of the palazzo. Choose your moment wisely."

Antonio, feeling the weight of the vial both in hand and in responsibility, nodded slowly. "This… this changes everything. Our chances have vastly improved."

The man smirked, his eyes alight with a certain malicious glee. "It does, indeed. But remember, Antonio, this isn't a tool to be wielded lightly. Misuse it, and the consequences can be… unpredictable."

Feeling a chill despite the warmth of the tavern, Antonio clutched the vial tighter. "I understand. I'll be cautious."

"Good," the figure responded, satisfaction evident in his voice. "Once you've secured the sapphire, meet me here. We'll then discuss our next steps, our path to power and riches beyond imagination."

As Antonio left the tavern, vial securely tucked away, his mind raced with possibilities. The allure of the sapphire, its power and value, tugged at him even more strongly now. The elixir, he felt, was the missing piece, the tool that would make his dangerous ambition a reality.

Yet, amidst his plans and dreams, a small voice, a remnant of his former self, whispered a warning. He remembered Liliana's gently touch, the warmth of her gaze. With the power to betray at his fingertips, the path ahead was fraught with moral dilemmas.

****

The darkness of the night was slashed by the silvery streak of the moon, which painted the facades of grand structures with its luminescent touch. Antonio stood just beyond the wrought iron gates of the Morosini Palazzo, a lute clutched close to his chest. His heart thudded, not just from the thrill of the impending theft but also from the emotional tightrope he was walking. Drawing a deep breath, he began to strum the instrument, its melancholic notes echoing in the stillness. His voice, rich and heartfelt, wove tales of love and longing, of desires unspoken and dreams unfulfilled.

Inside the palazzo, Liliana sat in her chamber, the pensive tranquility of the night broken by the faintest strains of a melody. Curiosity sparked, she moved to the window, drawing aside the heavy drapes. The sight that met her eyes cause her heart to flutter - there, in the moonlit gardens, stood Antonio, serenading her. The sheer romanticism of the gesture rendered her speechless.

The tender lyrics spoke of a love that dared to reach out, even in the face of adversity. Each note seemed to caress her very soul, making her forget the grandeur of her surroundings and focus solely on the man whose voice now filled every corner of her heart.

Lost in the music, she descended the staircase, her silken night robe flowing behind her like a river of moonlight. She opened the grand doors, stepping into the courtyard, where Antonio's voice grew clearer, more poignant.

Their eyes met, and the world around them seemed to

dissolve. Antonio approached, the last notes of his song echoing away, leaving behind a silence laden with emotion.

"Liliana," he whispered, the intensity of his gaze unwavering.

"Antonio," she replied, her voice barely audible, the weight of the moment pressing upon her. "Your song… it's beautiful. It touched my very soul."

He smiled, taking a step closer. "It was but a reflection of the beauty I see before me, the beauty that has captured my heart."

Moved by his words, Liliana extended her hand, inviting him inside. "Come, let us not stand out here in the cold. Share with me a drink, and perhaps another song?"

Antonio hesitated for a mere moment, the weight of his true intent pulling at him, but then with a gentle nod, he accepted. They moved together through the palazzo's grand entrance, the looming walls and arches standing as silent witnesses to the unfolding drama.

Inside, they settled in the main lounge, a room adorned with opulent tapestries and gilded furniture. A servant was summoned, and soon, goblets filled with ruby-red wine were presented.

As they sipped their drinks, the conversation flowed effortlessly. They reminisced about their shared moments, the boat rides and picnics, the operas, and the shared glances. But as the night deepened, so did Antonio's internal conflict. Every time Liliana's laughter filled the room, or her hand brushed against his, the weight of his deceit pressed harder upon his chest.

Liliana, her guard completely down, revealed in the

intimacy of the moment. "Antonio," she began, her gaze searching his face, "it feels as though our souls have known each other for lifetimes. There's a familiarity, a connection that's hard to put into words."

Antonio, his throat tight, managed to reply, "I feel it too, Liliana. It's as if our paths were destined to cross." Yet, as the night wore on, Antonio began to feel the walls closing in. He would need to act soon, but the question remained - could he betray the trust of a woman who had opened her heart and home to him?

As the evening deepened, the flicker of candles lent a warm, amber hue to the room, shadows danced on the walls, weaving tales of intrigue. The sound of soft music from a distant corner, coupled with the warmth of the wine, created an atmosphere of intimacy. Each story shared, every lingering glance, drew Liliana and Antonio closer. Yet, amidst the allure of the moment, Antonio's mind raced.

Liliana, lost in conversation, recounted tales of her ancestors, their valour, and their legacy. Antonio, feigning interest, waited for the opportune moment to present itself. And when it did, he seized it. Complaining of a sudden ailment, perhaps the aftereffects of the night's wine, he excused himself.

"I may have drunk a tad too much," he grimaced, placing a hand to his temple. "Perhaps some fresh air will aid."

Liliana, her brow creased in concern, urged him to rest. "Take all the time you need," she whispered, her voice laced with worry.

Slipping away from the lounge, Antonio navigated the winding corridors of the palazzo. The weight of the vial pressed against his chest from within the confines of his cloak. Drawing it out, he held it to the dim light, the liquid within glinting malevolently. With one last look to ensure he wasn't observed, he uncorked the vial, allowing its contents to mingle with the air. A silvery mist formed, delicate yet deadly, wafting through the palazzo.

In its wake, guards stationed at various posts slumped, rendered unconscious by the potent concoction. Their breathing was even, their state mimicking a deep slumber. They would be unharmed, but incapacitated long enough for Antonio to achieve his sinister objectives.

With stealth, he approached the chamber where the heirloom was rumoured to be kept. The door, ornately carved with scenes depicting the Morosini lineage, stood imposingly before him. Drawing a set of lock picks for his pocket, he set to work. Each click, every subtle movement, was a testament to his expertise as the lock yielded.

As the door creaked open, he was met with a sight that left him momentarily breathless. The room, bathed in moonlight, seemed to pulsate with an ethereal glow. At its heart, on a pedestal of pure marble, lay the sapphire. The gem, even in the muted light, shone with an inner fire, its facets reflecting dreams of power and riches.

Moving closer, Antonio could feel its pull, an almost magnetic allure. It wasn't just the value of the stone but the legends that surrounded it, the power it was rumoured to possess. With trembling hands, he reached out, his fingers mere inches from its cool surface.

But fate, often unpredictable, had other plans. The haunting quiet of the room was punctuated by the distant muffled shuffle of footsteps. Antonio's heart skipped a beat. Every fiber of his being screamed of imminent danger. Was he discovered? In the vast expanse of the palazzo, a sound so fain't shouldn't have been discernible, but in this intense moment, his senses were heightened.

Torn between desire and prudence, he hesitated for what felt like an eternity. Just as he made the audacious choice to pocket the sapphire and face the repercussions, a voice, cold and cutting, sliced through the tense air.

"Antonio?"

It was Giovanni. He stood there, silhouetted against the soft glow filtering in through a distance window, his gaze piercing Antonio like a dagger.

Caught in the act, Antonio's facade crumbled. His usual charm and eloquence deserted him, replaced by an awkward stammer. "Giovanni… I… I can explain…"

But Giovanni wasn't in a mood for explanations. His stance, rigid with anger and disappointment, bore testimony to that. "Explain? How do you explain betrayal, Antonio? All for this… this *trinket?*" Giovanni's voice dripped with disdain as he gestured towards the sapphire.

Feeling cornered, Antonio's survival instincts kicked in. "It's not what you think, Giovanni. I… I was simply enamoured by its beauty. I meant no harm."

Giovanni's cold laughter echoed through the chamber. "Enamoured? And I supposed the incapacitated guards outside were also victims of your… affection?"

The atmosphere grew thick with tension. Their eyes locked, a silent battle of wills ensuing. Antonio, realising that words would no longer serve him, braced himself for what might come next. Giovanni, though slighter in stature, possessed a strength and determination that belied his appearance.

****

Liliana's heart raced as she approached the source of the disturbance. The sound of raised voices echoed through the palazzo's intricately decorated halls. Upon entering, her gaze instantly landed on the two figures - her brother, fierce and unyielding, and Antonio, the man she thought she knew, looking defeated and cornered. The scene before her painted a vivid picture: Antonio, attempting to steal their family's most treasured heirloom.

"Antonio?" Liliana's voice, usually melodic, came out as a broken whisper. Betrayal, like a sharp knife, cut deep, and her eyes mirrored the storm of emotions churning within her. "Is this what our time together meant to you? A mere ruse?"

Antonio, still reeling from his confrontation with Giovanni, now found himself facing an even greater challenge. The weight of Liliana's stare, her pain evident in her eyes, bore down on him. "Liliana…" he began, struggling to find the right words. "I won't lie. When I first met you, it was the sapphire that drew me in, its legend, its value. But as I got to know you, the person you are, my intentions shifted. What I feel for you now… it's real."

Giovanni, though simmering with rage, took a step back, allowing his sister to confront her suitor. The dynamic of the room shifted palpably. Where anger and defiance once dominated, vulnerability and raw emotion now took centre stage.

Liliana, tears glistening in her eyes, seemed to study Antonio for a long moment. "You expect me to believe that? After everything?" The anguish in her voice echoed the depths of her heartbreak.

Antonio, desperation evident in his posture, stepped closer, arms outstretched, seeking solace, seeking forgiveness. "Liliana, I won't deny my initial intentions. I came here with a purpose, a dark purpose. But every moment I spent with you changed me. Your grace, your kindness, the love that you showed… it made me question everything, every dark path I had walked on."

A heavy silence enveloped the room. The two of them, locked in a gaze, seemed to converse without words, conveying pain, betrayal, hope, and a plea for understanding. The sapphire, the bone of contention, lay forgotten for a moment, its glow dimmed in comparison to the raw emotions on display.

Giovanni's voice dropped to a whisper, lethal in its calmness, finally intervening. "Leave Venice, and pray that I never lay eyes on you again."

Antonio, nodding slowly, turned to leave but not before whispering, "I truly am sorry, Liliana. If there's any part of you that still believes in us, in what we had… remember that amidst all the deceit, my feelings for you were the only true thing."

And with that, he was gone, leaving behind a trail of shattered dreams and a heartbroken heiress grappling with the layers of deceit and genuine affection.

****

The grand meeting room of the Morosini Palazzo, typically reserved for celebrations and grand occasions, now bore witness to a different kind of gathering. The long, mahogany table, once a symbol of the family's unity and prosperity, felt cold and unwelcoming. The tall, arched windows with their intricate stained-glass patterns barely let in the moonlight, casting a subdued, eerie glow on the faces of the assembled family members.

Leonora sat at the head of the table, her posture regal and composed. But the lines of stress on her face betrayed her true feelings. To her right, Giovanni, still seething from the altercation, wore an expression of grim determination. Liliana, on the other hand, looked like a shadow of her former self. The vibrant woman, who just days before, was the epitome of happiness and grace, now seemed crushed, her eyes downcast and her spirit seemingly broken.

Also present were other close family members, including a few trusted cousins and elders, whose wisdom was frequently sought in times of crisis. Everyone understood the gravity of the situation. The heirloom wasn't merely a gem; it was a symbol of their legacy, their heritage. The betrayal wasn't just of Liliana's heart; it was a stab at the very soul of the Morosini name.

"We must act, and we must act swiftly," Giovanni began, his voice firm. "Antonio's betrayal is a stain on our honour. We cannot, under any circumstances, allow this engagement to continue."

A murmur of agreement swept the room. But all eyes turned to Liliana, awaiting her response. After a deep breath, she spoke, her voice surprisingly stead, "I loved him, or I believed I did. But I cannot, in good conscience, bind our family's fate to a man whose intentions were so tainted. I agree with Giovanni. The engagement must be broken."

Leonora, nodding gravely, added, "The Morosini name stands for honour, integrity, and trust. We will not allow it to be sullied by deceit and treachery. We must send a clear message that such betrayal will not be tolerated."

A senior family elder, a venerable figure with a long white beard and piercing blue eyes, leaned forward, "We must, however, also reflect upon this. How did we come to this point? How did we let someone with such intentions come so close? We need to be vigilant, not just for the sake of our heirloom, but for our future, our children's future."

The room echoed with a chorus of agreement. It was clear that the family was united in its decision.

Leonora took a deep breath and declared, "Then it's decided. The engagement between Liliana and Antonio will be officially broken off. We will draft a statement and ensure it reaches every corner of the land. Let this serve as a reminder and a lesson."

As the family members rose from their seats, the weight of the evening's decisions heavy on their shoulders, a renewed sense of unity and purpose emanated from them.

****

The opulence of Liliana's chamber seemed dull in the

dim candlelight, each flicker casting ethereal shadows on the room's rich tapestries and frescoes. A magnificent four-posted bed with lush drapery stood on one side, and near a window overlooking the expansive Morosini gardens was a rosewood writing desk, currently strewn with parchments, quills, and an ornate inkwell.

The room echoed of Liliana's state of mind, a stark contrast between its inherent beauty and the turmoil that now enveloped her. Seated by the desk, her fingers trembling slightly, she picked up a quill. The parchment beneath seemed so vast, like an expanse waiting to be filled with the depths of her feelings.

The candlelight glinted off her tear-brimmed eyes as she began to write, each word a testament to her raw emotions:

Dearest Antonio,

The quill shakes in my hand as I pen this, for the heart it represents trembles too. Our story, which I once believed was scripted among the stars, now feels like a tragic play. How do I reconcile the Antonio who made my heart soar with the man whose actions have now rooted it in despair?

When I looked into your eyes, I saw a future. I saw laughter, shared dreams, and whispered secrets under moonlit skies. But now, all I see is the shadow of deceit, lurking behind every stolen glance and sweet word. How can love and betrayal reside so closely in one heart?

You may wonder why I write, especially since my family and I have decided our paths must now diverge. It is because, amidst the anger and the hurt, there remains a part of me that needs closure, that needs to voice the pain of a dream shattered. It's not to seek answers or justifications but to give voice to a love that once was pure and unattained.

I once believed our souls were intertwined, that our destinies were inseparably linked. But now, I must sever those ties, for the path you chose is not one I can tread alongside you. Our story, Antonio, ends here. But before it does, I wanted you to know the depth of my feelings - the love, the hurt, the confusion.

Perhaps, in another lifetime, our tale could have been different. But in this one, it ends with this unsent letter, with words that you might never read but that I needed to pen. It ends with a goodbye, not just to you, but to the dreams and hopes we once shared.

Forever in my heart, but no longer in my life,
Liliana

As she finished the letter, the weight of her emotions threatened to crush her. Folding the parchment delicately, she sealed it with wax, bearing the family crest. She looked at it for a long moment, the finality of her actions sinking in. And then, with a resolve born out of pain and the need to move forward, she placed the letter in a drawer, locking away not just the words but the chapter of her life that had just ended.

In that simple act, Liliana signalled her intent. She would cherish the memories but was resolved to move forward, leaving behind the shadows of betrayal and embracing the promise of a new dawn.

Chapter 7

At the heart of the grand Morosini Palazzo, Leonora's laughter had often echoed through the hallways, her wise words often serving as the beacon guiding the family through treacherous times. Her very presence was a comforting blanket, assuring everyone that as long as she was there, all would be well.

But of late, that beacon seemed to flicker. The laughter was replaced by a contemplative silence, and the corridors of the palazzo echoed with a stillness that made even the bravest hearts uneasy.

The dining hall, which once buzzed with conversations and heart meals, bore the brunt of this exchange. Leonora, seated at the head of the long oak table, seemed distant. Her meals were often left untouched, her gaze fixed on a point beyond the realm of the room. Family discussions, which she once led with vigour, now went on with her contributing little to nothing. It was as if her mind wandered realms far away from the immediate concerns of her family and their estate.

Liliana was the first to voice her concerns. "Has mother seemed… different to you lately?" she whispered to Giovanni one evening, as they both noticed Leonora absentmindedly tracing patterns on the tablecloth, lost in a world of her own.

Giovanni, typically stoic and reserved, nodded slowly. "I thought it was just the weight of the recent events taking a toll on her. But this… this seems more profound."

Their conversations weren't isolated. Throughout the sprawling palazzo, in hushed tones and behind closed doors, the same concerns were being shared. Servants exchanged worried glances as Leonora walked past, her steps lacking their once purposeful stride. Relatives, during their occasional visits, would leave with a furrowed brow, the joviality of their meetings overshadowed by the palpable change in the matriarch.

Liliana tried to breach the wall that seemed to have formed around Leonora. With a tray of her favourite pastries, she approached her in the drawing room. "Mother," she began, trying to infused warmth into her voice, "you've barely eaten today. I thought you might like some of these."

Leonora's gaze shifted to meet her daughter's eyes. There was a brief moment, a flicker, where the old Leonora - full of warmth and love - seemed to return. But just as quickly, it vanished, replaced by the same distant look. "Thank you, Liliana," she said, her voice soft, almost a whisper, "Maybe later."

Heart heavy, Liliana retreated, leaving the tray on a nearby table. As she exited the room, she couldn't shake off the feeling that the mother she knew was slipping away, replaced by a version she couldn't quite recognise.

The family, while concerned, hoped it was a phase. Perhaps it was the weight of the responsibilities, the constant decisions, or the recent betrayal they had faced. But as days turned to weeks, the transformation became undeniable. Leonora was changing.

She would often retreat to the chamber that locked away

the sapphire at odd hours, her figure silhouetted against the dim light of the hallway as she entered. Inside, the sole source of illumination was a candle whose flame danced erratically, casting shadows that played upon the walls, making the room come alive in a macabre performance. At its centre stood the display containing the sapphire, its deep blue depths gleaming mysteriously.

One of the older servants had been in the corridor late one evening when she heard it: a low, murmurous whisper emanating from behind the chamber's doors. Thinking that the matriarch might need assistance, she had approached, only to realise that Leonora seemed to be talking to herself. Or perhaps, to the sapphire. Her words were indistinguishable, but the tone was clear - it was a mix of plea, command, and reverence.

Word of this unusual behaviour spread throughout the household, fuelling a mix of concern and dread among the staff. Theories began to form: was the Lady Morosini communing with spirits? Or had the stress finally taken a toll, causing her to lose touch with reality?

And then there were her rare appearances outside the chamber. When she emerged, Leonora seemed transformed. No longer the distant, contemplative woman of the past weeks, she exuded an aura of raw power. Her eyes, previously lost in thought, now pierced with an intensity that made even the bravest souls look away. Her walk, her voice, her very presence felt magnified, leaving an impression long after she left a room.

During a breakfast gathering, her newfound assertiveness was unmistakably evident. As debates about the family's future and finances arose, she silenced the room with a single, commanding gesture. "The Morosini legacy is mine to protect," she declared, her voice rising with authority, "and I will ensure its rise to unparalleled heights."

Giovanni, trying to bridge the growing chasm, gently interjected, "Mother, we only wish to understand the decisions-"

She cut him off with a withering look. "You will understand in due time," she retorted sharply, leaving no room for further discussion.

Liliana, watching from across the table, felt a pang of sorrow. The mother she had once confided in, sought advice from, and laughed with, now seemed a stranger. The heartache of Antonio's betrayal still fresh, she found herself grappling with another loss - the undeniable change in her mother.

As days turned into nights and nights into days, the palazzo seemed to echo with whispered conversations and hushed concerns. The once cohesive Morosini clan now felt splintered, with Leonora's behaviour driving a wedge between family members.

****

Members of the Morosini clan took their seats around the expansive wooden table. Candles flickered, illuminating faces that mirrored concern, uncertainty, and expectancy. At the head of the table sat Leonora, the sapphire pendant around her neck glinting in the dim light. Her eyes scanned the room, acknowledging each family member with a measured gaze.

"Good evening," she began, her voice carrying the confidence that had become her trademark of late. "There are ventures I believe our family should pursue. Ventures that promise untold riches and power beyond our wildest dreams."

She proceeded to lay out her proposals, speaking of business endeavours in far-off lands and potential alliances with factions that the Morosinis had previously deemed untrustworthy. Her words painted a future of immense wealth and dominance, but with undertones of risks that seemed to carelessly dance on the precipice of disaster.

There was a heavy silence as she concluded. The family exchanged uneasy glances, the weight of Leonora's words sinking in.

Giovanni was the first to break the silence. "Mother, while your vision is admirable, these endeavours carry risks that can jeopardise our legacy. And these alliances," he paused, choosing his words carefully, "they are with people who have wronged us in the past. How can we trust them now?"

Leonora's gaze turned icy. "Because, Giovanni, times change. Power dynamics shift. The world respects strength and audacity. We cannot be shackled by old feuds and past slights."

Liliana attempted to bridge the growing divide. "Perhaps there's a middle ground, Mother. Ventures that promise growth but with calculated risks."

Leonora's eyes flashed. "Middle ground? Compromises have never been the Morosini way."

Giovanni, his frustration evident, rose from his seat. "The Morosini way has always been about protecting our name and legacy, not personal ambitions. I cannot, in good conscience, support these endeavours."

The room bristled with tension, the family clearly divided. Some, swayed by Leonora's vision of unparalleled power, seemed included to support her. Yet, others, led by Giovanni's cautionary stance, resisted. Voices rose in heated debate, arguments punctuated with both reason and emotion.

Leonora, sensing the resistance, remained unyielding. "Those who stand with my will witness the dawn of a new Morosini era. Those who oppose can stay mired in the past."

Giovanni's face turned a shade paler, his love and respect for his mother evident, but so was his alarm at the path she was treading. "Mother, it's not about the past. It's about safeguarding our future."

Leonora leaned back, the glint of the sapphire catching the candlelight just so, casting a blueish hue across her once familiar visage. Her eyes, once full of maternal warmth, now seemed distant and calculating. "The future, my dear Giovanni, is shaped by those brave enough to seize opportunities. It is shaped by visionaries, not by those paralysed by fear."

Giovanni's eyes darted to the sapphire, then back to his mother's face, searching for the woman who had once held him during storms, whispering assurances. "This isn't about bravery, Mother. It's about wisdom. There's a difference between seizing opportunities and recklessly bartering away our family's legacy."

Leonora's voice took on a note of sharpness, a stark contrast to her usually melodious tone. "And who, precisely, has deemed your perspective as wisdom? Is it not possible that you simply lack the foresight to understand the grandeur of what I envision?"

There was a painful pause, filled only by the soft crackling of the fireplace. Liliana, witnessing the escalating rift between her mother and brother, tried to intervene. "Perhaps we can find an external counsel? Seek opinions outside of our family, maybe they could offer an unbiased viewpoint?"

Leonora shot her a quick, dismissive glance. "The Morosini matters remain with the Morosini walls. We do not seek validation from outsiders."

Liliana's expression saddened, her efforts to mediate rebuffed. "All I'm suggesting is a perspective that might bridge our divides. Mother, Giovanni only wishes to preserve our family's honour."

Giovanni nodded in agreement. "Thank you, Liliana. Mother, all I ask is that we weigh the pros and cons thoroughly. The risks you're suggesting are enormous."

Leonora rose from her seat, her silhouette towering. "This discussion is over. I have listened, I have spoken, and now I shall act. The Morosini legacy is in my hands, and I am determined to elevate it to heights hitherto unseen."

The air was thick with unspoken sentiments. Resentment, confusion, concern, and fear intertwined, casting a shadow over the family bond that had once been unbreakable.

Giovanni, his voice soft now but firm in resolve, spoke up, "I hope, Mother, that in your quest for greatness, you do not lose sight of what truly matters."

With that, he turned and walked away, leaving a room filled with tension, unsaid words, and a palpable sense of foreboding.

****

Liliana and Giovanni found solace in the privacy of the estate's expansive library. Surrounded by centuries-old manuscripts, tomes, and scrolls, the siblings could discuss their concerns without fear of prying ears.

Giovanni, looking even more worn than usually, began, "Liliana, we can't continue like this. Every day she grows more distant, more consumed. The sapphire isn't just a gem; there's something else tethered to it."

Liliana nodded in agreement, her eyes shimmering with unshed tears. "I've noticed too. Mother was never so… obsessive. We need to understand the sapphire's true nature."

Giovanni, rubbing his temples, replied, "Which is why we need someone who can dive deep into its past, without arousing suspicion."

Liliana's face brightened slightly, "There's Master Elric. Here's discreet and well-versed in ancient relics and their histories."

Giovanni recalled the elderly scholar, a man of few words but profound wisdom. "Yes, Elric. I trust him. We need to understand if there's a way to counteract the stone's influence."

Liliana, her hope rekindled, quickly penned a note. "I'll

ensure this reaches him without delay. He's helped our family with discretion in the past. He understands the importance of confidentiality."

As the note was sent off, carried by a trusted servant into the window streets beyond the estate, the siblings poured over any existing records about the heirloom. Their search, however, was limited. The Morosini archives had very little on the sapphire, save for its immense value and the year it was acquired.

Giovanni frowned, "it's as if the history before our family's initial possession was deliberately erased or hidden."

Liliana, her fingers brushing a particularly old ledger, sighed, "Or perhaps our ancestors didn't want to delve too deep. Maybe they sensed its dangers and were content just possessing it."

Days turned into restless nights. The palazzo seemed to pulse with an undercurrent of anxiety. Servants tread lightly, exchanging worried glances, their whispers echoing the family's concerns.

In Leonora's private chambers, the sapphire's glow seemed to become more vibrant, its pull stronger. It wasn't just a gem, it had become an entity, a force that was steadily changing the dynamics of the family's household.

Outside her door, Liliana and Giovanni would often pause, placing their ears against the polished wood, trying to decipher their mother's late-night mutterings. All they heard were murmurs, undecipherable, yet laden with intent.

In one of these instances, Liliana turned to her brother, her voice quivering, "We're running out of time, Giovanni. I fear what might happen if Master Elric doesn't provide us with some insights soon."

Giovanni, his face a mask of determination, replied, "We will find a way, Liliana. We've faced many storms. We will weather this one too." In his heart, doubt gnawed at him. This wasn't an external enemy they battled, but one that resided within their very walls.

****

The Morosini siblings found themselves in Giovanni's study, a haven of books, parchments, and antique desks. The atmosphere was thick with apprehension as Liliana handed over the sealed envelope bearing Master Elric's familiar insignia. The wax seal was marked with the emblem of a quill intersecting an ancient scroll, symbolising Elric's lifelong devotion to the pursuit of knowledge.

Breaking the seal, Giovanni began to read aloud, his voice echoing off the cold marble floors. Liliana's eyes widened with each revelation.

"To the esteemed Morosini siblings,

Upon receiving your request, I embarked on a meticulous journey through the annals of history, uncovering tales both wondrous and foreboding about the sapphire you possess.

One account from the 12th century details the rise of a mere courtier to the stature of an influential duke within a span of mere months. However, the same man, intoxicated by aspirations of even grander dominions, initiated a rebellion against his king. He was captured, and met a gruesome end. Notably, at the height of his power, he was known to always carry the sapphire close.

A century later, a famed musician, her voice said to enchant all who heard it, came into possession of the stone. Rumours spoke of her mesmerising performances becoming increasingly powerful, ensnaring the will of her listeners. But it wasn't enough. She sought to dominate, to control, to be worshipped, leading to her eventual exile from society. Alone and desolate, her end came shrouded in sorrow and madness.

These stories, my dear Morosinis, are but a glimpse into the pattern that emerges. The sapphire, it appears, does not merely bestow power. It feeds and magnifies the deepest desires, ambitions, and even the darkness within its possessor. As radiant as the gem might be, its brilliance comes at a cost. An insatiable thirst for more power, more influence, to the point of one's own undoing.

Guard yourselves and your beloved mother. History, if not acknowledged, is doomed to repeat itself.

Yours in knowledge and service,
Master Elric."

The weight of Master Elric's revelations hung heavily in the air. Liliana, her face pale, whispered, "Giovanni, we can't let mother continue down this path. We must do something."

Giovanni, placing the letter carefully on his desk, turned to his sister. "I know, Liliana. We have our work cut out for us. We must find a way to either harness or negate the sapphire's influence."

Liliana took a deep breath, her resolve firming, "We've

lost Antonio to his treachery, we cannot afford to lose our mother to the whims of this cursed stone."

The chamber's ornate clock chimed, marking the passing of another hour. Time was of the essence, and the Morosini siblings knew that they stood on the precipice of potential calamity. The road ahead was fraught with uncertainty, but one thing was clear: they would face it together.

Their unity, however, would be tested sooner than anticipated. A commotion at the door was followed by the entrance of their trusted family steward, Alessandro, who bore the look of a man burdened with grave tidings. "Signor Giovanni, Signorina Liliana," he began with a slight quiver in his voice, "I regret to bring such news in an already turbulent time, but there's a matter requiring immediate attention."

Without waiting for a response, he unfolded a parchment and began to read its contents. "Lady Leonora has decreed the sale of vast tracts of our ancestral lands - the vineyards of Casa Morosini, the love groves of Montefiore, and the pastures of Valdorria."

Liliana gasped, her hand flying to her mouth. These lands weren't just sources of revenue; they bore the legacy of countless Morosini generations. "To whom?" she managed to utter.

Alessandro hesitated before replying, "To the consortium led by the Grimaldi family for a venture in the East. They promise wealth beyond imagination, gold from the farthest realms."

Giovanni's eyes darkened. The Grimaldis were a notorious family, known more for their cunning and treachery than their business acumen. "A venture in the East? At what cost? Do they not know the dangers that lurk in those uncharted territories?"

"The exact details remain shrouded in mastery," Alessandro said, "but whispers suggest it involves the Silk Route, with promises of opening newer, richer avenues of trade."

Liliana's heart raced. "This isn't like Mother. These lands… they're our history, our soul! How could she part with them so easily?"

Giovanni, trying to piece things together, speculated, "The sapphire. Its influence over her seems to be growing. Amplifying her desires, making her take risks she wouldn't have dreamt of before."

Liliana nodded, her fears reflected in her brother's eyes. "We must confront her. Try to make her see reason."

Giovanni stood, determination etched on his face. "Yes, but cautiously. We must tread carefully, understanding the depth of the sapphire's grip on her. We cannot risk pushing her further away."

The siblings exchanged a meaningful look, their eyes echoing the same sentiments. It was becoming painfully evident that the greatest threat to the Morosini lineage wasn't looking from some external adversary but was festering from within its very core. They were racing against time, not just to save the treasures and prestige of their house, but to salvage the very essence of their mother from the clutches of the malevolent sapphire.

Giovanni, his patience wearing thin and frustration evident, sought out his mother in her private chambers. The heavy wooden doors swung open to reveal Leonora, her figure silhouetted against the room's dim lighting, her eyes fixed intently on the glittering sapphire.

Without any preamble, he began, "Mother, what are you doing? Selling our lands, our heritage? To the Grimaldis, no less! Have you lost all reason?"

Leonora slowly turned to face him, her usually soft features now hardened, an eerie confidence emanating from her. "Giovanni, my dear son, you see just the surface. The sapphire has shown me visions, grand visions of our family. The Morosinis won't just be one among the noble houses of Venice. We will be *the* noble house. Dominating, dictating, reigning supreme. And I," her voice grew stronger and more passionate, "I will be the beacon leading us to that destiny."

Giovanni, taken aback by the intensity in her voice, tried to reason. "Mother, our ancestors built our legacy with care and respect for our traditions. You risk it all for a dream, a mere illusion?"

Leonora's laughter filled the room, cold and devoice of the warmth Giovanni remembered. "It's not an illusion, my son. It's a prophecy. And I will see it fulfilled."

Giovanni's temper flared, but he tempered it with concern. "Mother, listen to yourself! This isn't you! You speak of prophecy and visions, but at what cost? Our heritage? Our honour? Do these mean nothing to you now?"

Leonora's face contorted into a sneer. "Honour? Heritage? Those are but chains that have bound our family for generations, preventing us from achieving our true destiny. The sapphire has awakened me to the possibilities, to the power that is rightfully ours!"

"Awakened? Or ensnared?" Giovanni shot back, his voice quivering with a mix of anger and desperation. "Look around you, Mother. The family is fracturing, and Venice is rife with whispers. They don't speak of our rising power; they speak of our impending doom."

Leonora's eyes flashed dangerously, her hands clenching at her sides. "So you listen to the idle chatter of the city, rather than your own mother? Perhaps you are the problem, Giovanni. Maybe you're the weak link that's been holding the Morosinis back."

Stung by her words, Giovanni stepped closer, his voice low and intense. "I do not heed the whispers of the city, but I will always listen to my heart. And my heart is screaming that we're losing you, that this sapphire is not a blessing but a curse. Liliana and I, we've seen its history, the ruin it brought upon its previous owners."

Leonora laughed again, this time louder, more mocking. "Stories, tales meant to frighten children. I am no child, Giovanni. And I am not afraid."

Giovanni's voice cracked, a tear glistening in his eye. "I am, Mother. I'm terrified. Not of the sapphire, but of what it's doing to you. Of the mother I'm losing. The Morosini legacy isn't about power or dominion; it's about family, love, honour. If we forsake that, we forsake everything."

The silence that followed was deafening. Mother and son locked eyes, each searching for a flicker of the love that had once bound them so closely. For a heartbeat, there was a softening in Leonora's gaze, but it vanished as swiftly as it appeared, replaced by the cold determination that had become her trademark.

“I’ve made my decision, Giovanni,” she declared icily. “You are either with me, or you stand in my way. Choose wisely.”

Giovanni, shattered by the chasm that now yanked between them, whispered, “I choose the Morosini family, Mother. Always.”

Leonora’s face remained impassive, her cold eyes never leaving her son’s devastated visage. “Then perhaps you should reconsider what the Morosini family stands for now.”

As those chilling words settled, the room’s temperature seemed to plummet, creating an almost tangible barrier between mother and son. The once-unbreakable bond they had shared now felt tenuous at best.

Giovanni gathered his composure. “If this is the path you choose, Mother, know that I will do everything in my power to protect this family from harm, even if that harm comes from within.” His voice, while steady, betrayed a raw pain that resonated in the echoing chamber.

Leonora responded with a smirk. “Then we are at an impasse. I see a future of limitless potential, while you cling to outdated ideals and sentiments.”

Giovanni squared his shoulders, his demeanour unyielding. “There is honour in this ‘outdated’ ideals, Mother. They have guided our family for centuries, helping us weather countless storms. Abandoning them now will only lead to our ruin.

Liliana, who had been observing the heated exchange silently from the shadows, stepped forward. Her voice, gentle yet firm, added, “Mother, we are not your enemies. We want what’s best for the family. Please, let’s find a way to come together."

Leonora's eyes darted between her two children, her expression momentarily unreadable. But then, with a sigh that hinted at weariness, she replied, "I have seen the path to greatness, my dear children. I cannot and will not divert from it."

Giovanni took a step closer, extending a hand. "Then let us walk that path together, Mother. Not as adversaries, but as a family. Let us find a middle ground."

But Leonora, her gaze returning to the glint of the sapphire, responded with a finality that left no room for negotiation. "I am afraid that is no longer possible."

Without another word, she turned and retreated from the room, leaving her children grappling with the stark reality of their fractured family and the looming storm on the horizon.

Chapter 8

The cobblestone streets of the city lay bathed in the dim glow of the lanterns, their golden lights flickering like subdued stars. It was a night when the world seemed to hold its breath, the skies above painted with shades of indigo and charcoal. Every footfall, every whisper of the wind, seemed magnified in the shroud of the night's silence.

Giovanni adjusted the collar of his cloak, pulling it tighter around him to shield against the evening chill. Tonight was not a night for being recognised, nor for casual encounters with acquaintances. There was an urgency in his step, a purpose that drove him forward, away from the grandeur of the Morosini estate and into the maze of the city's lesser-known streets.

As he moved, his mind was a tempest of thoughts, the foremost of which was Matteo. The very thought of him brought a warmth to Giovanni's heart, a sharp contrast to the cold cobblestones beneath his feet. In a world that often felt constrictive and judgmental, Matteo was Giovanni's sanctuary. Their love, hidden from the world's prying eyes, was a flame that burned fiercely, fuelled by stolen moments and secret rendezvous..

Tonight, Giovanni had news to share, a dream to paint for their future. He'd been contemplating it for weeks, and tonight, he would reveal it to Matteo. They would find a place away from the suffocating grip of the city, away from whispered judgments and societal expectations. A place where love wasn't cloaked in shadows, where they could simply *be*.

He deftly navigated the alleyways, his knowledge of the city's hidden corners serving him well. Occasionally, he'd catch the eye of a stray cat or hear the distant hum of a lullaby being sung, but he moved with a practiced stealth, ensuring he left no trail.

An internal monologue unfurled within him, "Matteo," he mused, "how the very essence of your name brings solace to my heart. How many times have we dreamt of a world where our love isn't the subject of hushed whispers? Tonight, I'll share my vision, our path to freedom." He imagined Matteo's eyes, deep and understanding, listening intently, their shared dreams of freedom intertwining like ivy.

Giovanni's heart raced, not from the exertion of his journey, but from the anticipation of seeing his lover. The weight of the city's expectations and the looming shadow of the Morosini legacy often felt suffocating. But with Matteo, those weights lifted, if only for stolen moments. Tonight's meeting promised more than just fleeting escapism; it held the hope of a shared future.

Distracted by his thoughts, he almost missed the familiar sign of the rose and dagger, their designated meeting spot for tonight. As Giovanni approached, memories of past rendezvous flooded his mind. Each secret meeting with Matteo was a tale of its own: whispers of love, shared dreams, stolen kisses. This tavern was a place where souls intermingled freely, where stories flowed as generously as the wine. But for Giovanni and Matteo, it was their haven, a world within a world where they could escape, even if briefly.

The door to the tavern creaked softly as Giovanni entered. The ambient glow of candles cast dancing shadows on the wooden walls, and the hum of hushed conversations provided a gentle backdrop. A minstrel played a lilting tune on his lute, notes of longing and love that seemed fitting for the night.

Giovanni's eyes scanned the room, searching for Matteo's familiar silhouette. He had hoped to spot that playful glint in Matteo's eyes or the hint of a smile that always greeted him. But tonight, his table was vacant. A twinge of unease tightened in Giovanni's chest. They had been meticulous in their plans, ensuring they would meet at the same time, away from prying eyes.

After ordering a goblet of wine to blend in, Giovanni settled into a corner, giving him a vantage view of the entrance. Perhaps Matteo was running late, he tried to assure himself. The city had its own rhythm, unpredictable and ever-changing. Maybe he got caught up with some errand, or perhaps he was taking extra precautions tonight, Giovanni mused.

As minutes turned into hours, the tavern's clientele started thinning out. The minstrel had packed up his lute, and the candle's wicks had burnt down, now merely flickering stubs. But Matteo was nowhere in sight. Giovanni's unease grew, morphing into a gnawing worry. This wasn't like Matteo; he had always been punctual, especially about their meetings.

An old bartender, noticing Giovanni's lingering presence

and the untouched goblet of wine, approached him. "Waiting for someone?" he queried, wiping down a mug.

Giovanni hesitated, then nodded. "Have you seen a young man, dark hair, about this tall?" he gestured, "Perhaps he came in earlier?"

The bartender scratched his chin thoughtfully. "Many come and go, especially on nights like these. But I can't say I've seen anyone matching that description tonight."

Giovanni felt a chill that wasn't from the night's cold. The thought that something might have happened to Matteo was unbearable. Pushing away the goblet, he rose. "Thank you," he murmured, leaving a coin on the table.

The streets, which had been a pathway of hope earlier in the night, now seemed labyrinthine and ominous. Giovanni quickened his pace, driven by an urgency he couldn't suppress. He had to find Matteo. They had other places, other memories, and Giovanni was determined to search each one. The weight of his family name, the looming problems with his mother, all faded in the backdrop. Tonight, his heart and soul had only one focus, one name - Matteo.

After searching a few more of their usual spots and coming up empty, Giovanni decided it was time to pry deeper. Given the clandestine nature of their relationship, directly inquiring about Matteo could risk exposing them both. Yet, the urgency he felt left him with little choice but to discreetly probe for any leads.

He began his inquiry at the local apothecary, where Matteo often visited to procure herbs for his ailing mother. The elderly apothecary, Mistress Elara, was known for her discretion. She recognised Giovanni immediately, giving him a knowing look.

"Master Giovanni," she greeted with a nod, her eyes glinting with curiosity. "What brings you here so late at night?"

"Good evening, Mistress Elara," he replied with a smile. "I was looking for someone. Perhaps you've seen him?"

She raised an eyebrow but said nothing. Giovanni described Matteo without using his name, hoping she would catch on without the need for further explanation.

She hesitated for a moment before replying, "He came by this afternoon, seemed hurried. But he didn't mention any plans for the evening."

Giovanni thanked her and pressed on, his worry increasing with every fruitless inquiry. The moon had climbed high in the sky, casting an ethereal glow over the city.

He next sought the fishmonger Matteo sometimes assisted in the mornings. The docks were almost empty save for a few weary fishermen wrapping up their late catches. Among them was old Nicolo, with his salt-crusted beard and weathered hands.

Nicolo looked up as Giovanni approached. "Eh, what brings a Morosini to the docks this late?"

Giovanni hesitated, choosing his words carefully. "I'm looking for a friend. You might know him. He helps you sometimes?"

Nicolo grunted, rubbing his chin thoughtfully. "Aye, he was here this morning. Said he had something important in the evening. Seemed excited. But I haven't seen him since."

The puzzle pieces weren't coming together. Everywhere he inquired, he received pieces of a story, but none of them led to Matteo. Feeling the weight of despair, he thought of the one place he hadn't checked yet - Matteo's residence.

Matteo lived in a poorer quarter, an area Giovanni wasn't familiar with. He had never been to Matteo's home, respecting his lover's privacy and understanding the potential dangers of a Morosini being seen in such a locality. But tonight, desperation drove him.

The narrow streets and cramped houses of the quarter were a stark contrast to the grandeur of the Morosini estate. Sounds of late-night merriment and squabbles echoed. Children ran about, even at this late hour, and laundry hung overhead, fluttering like nocturnal ghosts.

After some searching and asking around, he found the dilapidated building Matteo called home. He hesitated outside the door, his heart heavy. This was a part of Matteo's life he had never been privy to. Pushing aside his reservations, he knocked.

A frail, elderly woman opened the door, her eyes widening in surprise upon seeing Giovanni. "Yes? How can I help you?"

"Good evening, madam," Giovanni began, his voice soft. "I am looking for Matteo. Is he home?"

The woman's expression changed, a mixture of confusion and sadness. "No, he's not. He left early in the evening. I thought he had work or was meeting friends. Why? Is something wrong?"

Giovanni bit his lip, his concern evident. "I was supposed to meet him tonight, but he didn't show. I've been looking for him everywhere."

The woman seemed worried. "That's unlike him. He always tells me if he's going to be late. I hope he's alright."

As Giovanni turned to leave, the weight of the night's events bore down on him. The cobblestone streets, which had always felt familiar, now seemed to twist and turn in confusing patterns, mirroring the turmoil within his heart. The sounds of the city faded into the background, and the silence within him grew louder, punctuated only by the unending echo of Matteo's name in his thoughts.

Matteo's mother's worry was evident in her eyes, and it mirrored Giovanni's own fear. Had he missed something? A hint or clue about where Matteo could be? They had always been so careful, meeting in secret places, sharing whispered conversations in the shadowy corners of the city. But had someone discovered their secret?

His thoughts were interrupted by a soft hand on his arm. He turned to see an old friend, Luciana, who lived a few houses away from Matteo. Her face, usually bright and vivacious, was marked with concern.

"Giovanni? What are you doing here at this hour? Is everything alright?"

He hesitated, weighing the consequences of confiding in her. But Luciana had always been trustworthy, a confidant during his younger, more reckless days.

"I was looking for Matteo," he confessed, his voice heavy. "He didn't meet me tonight, and no one seems to know where he is."

Luciana's face paled. "Giovanni, there were whispers, rumours about a man found by the canals earlier tonight. No one knows who he is, but the city guard was there, and there's been talk of foul play."

Giovanni felt his heart drop. "Take me there," he implored, his voice barely above a whisper.

Luciana nodded, leading him through the streets of the city. As they reached the canals, a small crowd had gathered, whispering among themselves. The city guard had cordoned off a section, and from his vantage point, Giovanni could see a lifeless form lying by the water's edge.

Pushing his way through, he approached the guard. "I need to see the body," he stated, trying to keep his voice steady.

The guard, recognising the Morosini heir, hesitated for a moment before reluctantly nodding. As Giovanni drew closer, he braced himself for the worst. The sight that meths eyes sent a shock through him; it was Matteo, his face pale in the moonlight, eyes forever closed in a deathly slumber.

Giovanni's knees buckled, and he would have fallen if not for Luciana's supportive arm. Tears blurred his vision as the weight of the realisation hit him. Matteo, his secret love, the one he had dreamt of a life away with, was gone.

Whispers circulated among the onlookers. Some speculated about the cause of death, while others murmured about the presence of a Morosini at such a scene. Luciana, sensing the increasing tension, gently urged Giovanni away.

As they walked back, Giovanni's mind was a whirlwind of emotions - grief, anger, confusion. But one thought stood out starkly among the rest: Who could have done this, and why?

Luciana tried to comfort him, but her words felt distant

and hollow. "I'm so sorry, Giovanni. We will find out what happened."

Luciana's words echoed in Giovanni's ears, but they provided little solace. The grim reality had begun to set in, making every step feel heavier than the last. They walked in silence, the city's hum slowly retreating into the backdrop of their own tumultuous emotions.

"Luciana," Giovanni whispered after a few moments, "who could want to harm Matteo? He was kind, gentle. He had no enemies."

She looked at him, her eyes searching his face for any sign of what he might already suspect. "This city," she began cautiously, "is a web of secrets, desires, and power plays. Sometimes, innocent souls get caught in the crossfire of larger schemes."

Giovanni clenched his fists. "But why him? Was it because of me? Because of our relationship?"

Luciana hesitated. "You both took precautions, but secrets, especially in Venice, have a way of surfacing. But making assumptions won't help. We need evidence, facts."

The thought of someone discovering their secret, using it against them, filled Giovanni with rage. "I will find out who did this," he vowed, the fierce determination evident in his eyes.

Luciana placed a comforting hand on his shoulder. "And I'll help you, Giovanni."

The next few days were a blur. Giovanni delved deep into the underbelly of Venice, seeking information about that fateful night. He frequented taverns, bribed informants, and even confronted known adversaries of the Morosini family, searching for any lead that might point him to Matteo's killer.

During his investigation, Giovanni discovered that on the night of Matteo's death, there had been a sighting of a cloaked figure near the canals. Although the identity was unknown, a distinct brooch in the shape of a raven was seen pinned to the cloak. This symbol was notorious in the city's underworld but was new information to Giovanni.

One evening, after another day of chasing shadows, Giovanni found himself in a dimly lit tavern. He was approached by an old woman with piercing blue eyes. Without introduction, she said, "The raven you seek is not what it seems. Look closer to home."

Before he could question her further, she disappeared into the crowd, leaving Giovanni both intrigued and disturbed by her cryptic message.

The following morning, a heavy mist hung over the city, reflecting Giovanni's own clouded thoughts. Luciana met him at their usual rendezvous spot. "Any progress?" she inquired.

Giovanni recounted his encounters and the old woman's words. Luciana paled upon hearing the description of the brooch. "I've seen it before," she whispered.

"Where?" Giovanni demanded.

She hesitated, taking a deep breath. "It belongs to a secret society within Venice, one that even the most powerful families tread lightly around. Their members are unknown, but they are believed to be involved in the city's most significant decisions."

The implications of her revelation were staggering. Was

Matteo's death connected to this society? Did the Morosini family, or even his mother, have any links to them?

Determined to unravel the mystery, Giovanni decided to confront the one person who might have answers - his mother, Leonora. But approaching her would mean risking everything, including revealing his secret love for Matteo. The stakes had never been higher.

****

The Morosini estate loomed large against the night sky, its silhouette ominous and foreboding. The sprawling mansion, usually a beacon of power and opulence, now seemed like a cage, hiding secrets Giovanni was desperate to unveil.

Giovanni knew the estate like the back of his hand, having grown up in its expansive corridors and lush gardens. But tonight, every shadow seemed suspicious, every rustling leaf a potential spy. His heart raced as he stealthily approached the residence, opting for a lesser-known entrance to avoid any unwanted confrontations.

Inside, the mansion was quiet, with only the soft glow of candles illuminating the long hallways. Giovanni navigated the familiar yet eerie corridors, making his way to Leonora's chambers. All the while, memories of happier times played in his mind, contrasting sharply with his current grim mission.

Reaching Leonora's door, Giovanni hesitated. The confrontation he was about to initiate could change everything. He took a deep breath, gathering his courage, and knocked softly. There was no response. He tried the handle, finding the door unlocked, and cautiously stepped inside.

The room was dimply lit, with an open window allowing the cool night breeze to waft in. At the far end, Giovanni could see the silhouette of his mother, Leonora, standing by the window, her gaze fixed on the city below.

"Mother," he began hesitantly, "we need to talk."

Leonora turned slowly to face him. Her usually commanding presence seemed diminished, her face bearing the weight of many sleepless nights. But her eyes, sharp and calculating, missed nothing.

"Giovanni," she replied, her voice cold and measured. "I was not expecting you."

"I have questions, and I need answers," Giovanni said, trying to keep his voice steady. "About Matteo."

Leonora's gaze did not waver. "What about him?"

"His death wasn't an accident, was it?" Giovanni pressed. "Someone wanted him dead. I need to know if our family, or even you, had any part in it."

Leonora's face remained impassive, but there was a hint of surprise in her eyes. "You think I had a role in your lover's demise?" she asked quietly.

Giovanni's heart ached at the mention of Matteo, but he steeled himself. "The brooch, the raven. It's connected to a secret society here in Venice, and I think you might be involved with it."

Leonora looked away for a moment, contemplating her next words. "You're delving into matters far beyond your understanding, Giovanni."

"But I deserve the truth!" Giovanni pleaded, the weight of his grief and frustration evident. "I loved him, Mother."

For the first time that night, a hint of emotion broke through Leonora's composed exterior. "And you think I don't know the pain of losing someone?" she shot back, her mind racing to memories of her late husband - Giovanni's father.

Giovanni was taken aback. "Then why? Why is he dead? And what is this society you're involved with?"

Leonora sighed, walking over to a table and pouring herself a drink. "The society you speak of has been a part of Venice for centuries, operating from the shadows, ensuring the city's prosperity. Sometimes, their methods and decisions are… questionable. But their motives are always for the greater good."

"And was Matteo's death for the 'greater good'?" Giovanni asked bitterly.

Leonora hesitated, her fingers tracing the rim of her glass. The room's atmosphere grew heavy, weighed down by the moment's significance. She finally looked up, her eyes searching Giovanni's, seeking understanding even in her confession.

"After everything this family has been through," she began slowly, "the last thing we needed was another scandal. I thought I was protecting our name, our legacy."

Giovanni's heart thudded loudly in his chest, his worst suspicions taking form. "You had him killed," he whispered, each word laden with disbelief and agony.

Leonora's gaze didn't waver. "I did it for the family. For our future."

"For the family?!" Giovanni's voice rose, cracking, filled with pain and anger. "Matteo was innocent! He was my love, my life! How could you?"

Leonora's face was a mask of pain and determination. "In the world we live in, Giovanni, love is a luxury. I did what I believed was necessary. The rumours, the whispers… they would have torn us apart."

"Love is a luxury?" Giovanni spat, eyes blazing with anger. "What you've done is monstrous! Matteo was worth a thousand of these shadowy games you play!"

Leonora's face crumpled, her facade breaking for a split second. "I truly believed I was doing what was best," she whispered. "I did not expect you to understand, but I hoped…"

"Hoped what? That I'd forgive you? That I'd move on?" Giovanni's voice trembled with rage. "You've taken everything from me. I will never forgive this."

Leonora reached out, trying to touch her son's arm, but he recoiled. "Giovanni…"

But he wasn't listening anymore. The revelations, the pain, and the betrayal consumed him, drowning out everything else. His world, once filled with love and hope, was now a landscape of ashes. Without another word, he turned on his heel, storming out of the room.

Leonora sank into a chair, he strength depleted. A single tear traced its way down her face. The prices of her decisions, she realised, was far higher than she had ever imagined. Her eyes drifted, not to the sapphire, but to the cloak that hung in the corner of her room, embedded within it a single raven brooch. Adjacent to it, the sapphire heirloom, which once promised power and prestige, now stood as a silent witness to the wreckage of a family torn apart by its own matriarch's choices.

Chapter 9

The grand halls of the Morosini estate, which once echoed with laughter and whispered secrets between siblings, now stood eerily silent. Every step Liliana took resonated through the vast chambers, her footsteps a stark contrast to the silent void that had descended upon the family home. The imposing walls, adorned with grand tapestries depicting tales of Morosini valor and grandeur, now felt oppressive, their threads weaving stories of a glorious past that seemed distant.

Each room, alive with memories of joyous feasts and celebratory gatherings, now lay in wait, untouched and cold. The once frequented sitting room, with its soft cushions and warm hearth, was a mere shadow of its former self, its fireplace flickering weakly, barely warding off the creeping chill. The grand dining hall, where stories flowed as seamlessly as wine, now bore witness to hushed conversations and hurried meals.

Liliana often found herself wandering these rooms, tracing her fingers over familiar furniture, as if trying to summon the spirits of happier times. Her heart ached at the realisation of how much had changed in such a short span of time. The disintegration was not loud or chaotic, but it was palpable. It was in the sidelong glances of servants who once smiled openly, in the terse nods exchanged between family members who used to share warm embraces.

By the tall, arched windows, she would pause, her eyes

surveying the vast gardens that stretched before her. The meticulously tended flowers stood tall and proud, their beauty unwavering. But where once the gardens echoed with the sounds of life - the playful banter of children, the soft strumming of lutes - now only silence reigned.

On one such introspective evening, as twilight cast long shadows, Liliana found herself in the manor's library. Surrounded by ancient scrolls and parchments, she traced the lineage of the Morosinis, reading of their deeds and aspirations. The inked words spoke of unity, pride, and love, so starkly contrasting the reality she now faced.

Closing the scroll, she felt an overwhelming weight, the burden of a legacy teetering on the edge. The parchment beneath her fingertips felt both fragile and enduring, a testament to a past that stood firm even as the present seemed to unravel.

She moved to the grand wooden table in the centre of the room, where a lone candle flickered, casting dancing shadows across the walls. The glow illuminated the faces of her ancestors, immortalised in hand-painted portraits that lined the room. They stared down at her, their expressions resolute and unyielding, as if urging her to find the strength to mend what had been broken.

She recalled tales she had heard as a child, whispered stories of Morosini unity, where family stood shoulder to shoulder, facing challenges as one. She longer for that unity, yearned for the support of her family in these trying times. But with Giovanni lost in his grief and her mother immersed in her ambitions, Liliana felt the onus rested upon her.

A soft sigh escaped her lips. She reached out, touching

the face of her grandmother in one of the portraits. The wise matriarch, with her piercing gaze, seemed to impart a silent message. The Morosinis had faced hardships before and it was their unity and unyielding spirit that had seen them through.

Drawing strength from the thought, Liliana straightened, her determination renewed. She may have felt alone in the sprawling estate, surrounded by silent stone and the watchful eyes of her ancestors, but she was not powerless. She would strive, she resolved, to mend the fractures that threatened her family, to reignite the warmth that once filled the halls of the Morosini palazzo.

With a newfound purpose, Liliana left the library, the soft glow of the candlelight fading behind her. She was no longer a mere observer of her family's descent but an active participant in its potential redemption. Each step she took echoed with the weight of her decision and determination. She could not simply stand by and watch the Morosini name be tarnished by greed and ambition. There was work to be done, and she intended to start immediately.

Reaching the main hall, servants bustled around, preparing for the evening's formal dinner. Silverware gleamed on the long wooden table, fresh roses adorned the centrepiece, and the air was perfumed with the scent of upcoming dishes. It was customary for the family to dine together at least once a week, an old tradition meant to fortify their bonds. But in recent times, these dinners had become mere formalities, filled with tense silences and veiled hostilities.

Liliana took a moment to oversee the preparations,

ensuring everything was in place. As the first family members began to drift into the hall, she took her position at one end of the table. It was a strategic decision, as it afforded her a view of everyone present.

Uncles, aunts, and cousins, each took their seats, exchanging polite nods and muted greetings. The Morosini dinners had always been a grand affair, a testament to their prominence in the society. Yet tonight, there was an underlying current of anxiety, a shared understanding that the family was at a pivotal crossroads.

Leonora entered last, her presence immediately commanding attention. She glanced around the room, nodding curtly to acknowledge the gathered family, and took her place at the head of the table opposite Liliana. Their eyes met for a brief moment, a silent exchange of defiance and challenge.

As servants began to bring forth the first course, the hall filled with the clinking of glasses and the muted murmur of conversation. Liliana took a deep breath, readying herself for the evening.

A parade of dishes emerged from the grand kitchen. The first, a delicately plated antipasto, was an assortment of thinly sliced cure meats, paired with marinated olives and sun-dried tomatoes. The vibrant colours danced on the plate, while the tantalising aroma of garlic, herbs, and rich oils wafted through the room, inviting salivating anticipation.

This was followed by a primi piatti of freshly made pasta. Spirals of tagliatelle drenched in a truffle-laden cream sauce. Each strand gleamed with the white decadence, intermingled with finely chopped herbs, promising a bite that was both earth and heavenly.

For the secondi, servers presented a magnificent roasted boar, its skin crackling and glistening, encrusted with rosemary and sage. Slices revealed succulent, aromatic meat that practically melted upon contact. It was complemented with roasted vegetables: bell peppers, zucchinis, and eggplants, charred to perfection, their smokiness offsetting the richness of the boar.

Dessert, the crowning glory, was a panna cotta so smooth it seems to shimmer under the chandeliers. Topped with a vibrant berry compote, its tartness provided the perfect counter to the creamy delicateness below.

As the meal progressed, family members indulged and marvelled, momentarily distracted from their worries. But it wasn't long before Leonora, her demeanour more assertive than ever, took the opportunity to steer the conversation towards her future aspirations.

"To the Morosini legacy!" she declared, raising her glass for a toast. The family followed suit, albeit some more hesitantly than others.

She began speaking of grand plans, of alliances with families previously deemed too risky to engage with, and ventures into territories and markets that the Morosini had historically steered clear of. "The age of sitting idly by, resting on the laurels of the our ancestors, is over," she proclaimed.

Every sentence dripped with ambition. She spoke of leveraging the might of the sapphire, of using its power to forge ahead in ways they'd never imagined. Tales of vast riches, of lands beyond their borders waiting to be claimed, and of the potential for the Morosini to not just influence but control trade routes and political landscapes.

Liliana's gaze swept the room, catching the expressions of her relatives. Some wore masks of polite agreement, while others, their brows furrowed, whispered anxiously among themselves. The matriarch's ambitious narrative had not gone unnoticed, and the hall, once alive with the joy of feasting, now hummed with unease.

Liliana tried to diffuse the tension. "Mother," she began gently, "we all want the best for our family. But perhaps we should consider the implications of these ventures? We have always held a reputation for our honour and ethics."

Leonora's eyes flashed, but her voice remained eerily calm. "Honour does not feed mouths, Liliana. Nor does it expand our legacy. I've seen the future of the Morosini, and it is grander than any of us can imagine."

Liliana, gathering her courage, rebutted. "Our legacy isn't just in riches and lands. It's in the love and unity of this family. If we lose that, what do we truly have?"

A tense silence blanketed the room. Leonora's gaze fixed on her daughter, a mix of incredulity and anger. "Our destiny is within grasp, and I will not see it squandered by sentimentality. If any do not wish to be a part of this future, they are free to leave."

Cousin Eduardo, always quick to sense where the wind was blowing, was the first to voice his support. "Leonora is right. Times are changing. We must adapt or be left behind."

Yet, for every nod of agreement, there were murmurs of descent. Uncle Francesco, who had built much of the family's trade routes, spoke up, his voice laced with worry.

"We mustn't forget our roots, our values. If we stray too far, we may never find our way back."

The dinner, meant to be a celebration, now teetered on the brink of chaos. Family members, once united, found themselves at crossroads, each torn between loyalty to the Morosini name and the fear of what lay ahead.

Liliana, seeing the rift widening, made a silent vow. She would find a way to heal the fractures, to remind her family of the ties that bound them.

In the days that followed, the vast halls and chambers of the Morosini estate saw a flurry of quiet activity. There was a strategic nature to Liliana's actions, the careful selection of those she chose to confide in and the discreet locations within the estate where these meetings took place. Sometimes it was in the old sunlit atrium, where the delicate sounds of a distant fountain masked whispered conversations. Other times, it was the secluded rose garden, where the scent of blooming flowers and the gentle rustling of leaves provided an intimate backdrop for discussions of loyalty and unease.

Each interaction was different, yet they all bore an undercurrent of concern. The once-resolute support for the Morosini matriarch had started to over among those who had always been staunch allies. They confided in Liliana, expressing reservations about the family's direction, apprehensions that mirrored her own. The aggressive ventures, the alliances with questionable characters - all these weighed heavily on their minds. The storied Morosini reputation, cultivated over centuries, seemed at risk.

While no words of outright rebellion were spoken, there

was a palpable desire for guidance and stability. A longing for the days when the family stood as a united front, undeterred by personal ambitions. There was an implicit trust in Liliana, a belief that she could be the beacon of hope and unity they so desperately sought.

Liliana took meticulous mental notes, piecing together a mosaic of sentiment and worry. With each conversation, she grew more resolute in her mission. The heart and soul of the family were at stake, and Liliana found herself unexpectedly thrust into the role of its protector. Every corridor she walked, every tapestry she passed, seemed to echo with the weight of responsibility. The ancient stones of the Morosini estate, which had borne witness to countless family dramas, now bore silent testimony to her quiet determination.

One evening, as dusk cast long shadows across the estate grounds, Liliana retreated to her private chambers. She felt a profound need to communicate, to seek guidance, and the only one who came to mind was Master Elric. With a heavy heart, she reached for her most prized parchment, the feathered quill, and a pot of the blackest ink. The same quill had documented many of the family's important decisions, and now, it would be a tool to express her deepest fears and hopes.

"Dearest Master Elric," she began, her script meticulous and steady, despite the turmoil in her heart. "The Morosini family finds itself on a precipice, and I fear we may fall if we do not find a way to right our path."

As the words flowed from the quill, a cascade of thoughts and emotions poured onto the parchment. She wrote of her mother's unsettling transformation, of her brother

Giovanni's heartbreak, and of the palpable tension that now permeated every room of their ancestral home.

She paused for a moment, looking at what she had written, the ink still glistening in the dim light. The act of laying bare her family's vulnerabilities brought clarity to her mind. The realisation was sudden and piercing: they couldn't merely wait and hope for things to improve. Waiting was a luxury they could no longer afford.

"With your wisdom and the breadth of your knowledge, I seek guidance," she continued. "How does one mend a family teetering on the edge of dissolution? How do we find our way back to the unity and purpose that once defined us?"

Closing her letter with a plea for any insights Master Elric might offer, Liliana felt a mix of vulnerability and resolve. Sending this letter was a risk, an open admission of the Morosini family's fragility. But it was a necessary step, one she hoped would help illuminate a path forward. With a wax seal stamped with the Morosini crest, she finalised her missive, entrusting it to the winds of fate.

The quiet stillness of the room seemed more pronounced after her fervent act of writing, the only sound being the faint crackle of the fireplace. The gravity of the family's predicament settled heavily upon her, and for a moment, she felt utterly alone.

Pushing the weighty thoughts to the back of her mind, Liliana decided to visit Giovanni. The hallways leading to his chambers were dimly lit, with long shadows flickering on the stone walls. Each step was heavy, laden with worry for her brother. The once proud and vibrant Giovanni had become a mere shadow of his former self, a transformation Liliana found deeply unsettling.

As she approached his door, she heard a soft melancholic tune emanating from within. Recognising the melody from their childhood, a lullaby their mother used to sing, Liliana felt a pang in her heart. Slowly, she pushed the door open to find Giovanni playing the tune on a lute, his eyes distant, lost in a world of memories and grief.

She moved closer, settling beside him. Words were unnecessary; the shared pain was evident. They sat in silence for what felt like an eternity, comforted by each other's presence, yet equally engulfed in their individual sorrows.

Reaching out, Liliana gently placed a hand on Giovanni's, causing him to stop playing. His eyes, red-rimmed and weary, met hers. In that moment, the depth of his pain was palpable. It was clear he was not yet prepared to face their mother, to deal with the harsh realities that lay ahead. The lute, his fingers, his very being seemed to cry out in despair. Liliana's heart ached for her brother, but she also recognised that they couldn't afford to be stagnant. Action was imperative.

Over the next few days, Liliana covertly reached out to those she felt could be trusted. The mansion's ornate chambers and garden alcoves became secret meeting spots, as whispered conversations took place under the cloak of night. From loyal family retainers to longstanding business associates, it was evident that Leonora's drastic change had not gone unnoticed.

In the dimly lit drawing room, surrounded by tapestries that told tales of Morosini valor, Liliana convened the first meeting of this new alliance. Each member had a personal stake in the family's future and shared Liliana's concerns about Leonora's reckless ambitions. It was a diverse group: Alessandro, the steward who had served the Morosini family for decades, Uncle Francesco, known for his sharp wit and network of informants thanks to his many years working in the trade industry, and the trusted guard Lorenzo, who had been disturbed by Leonora's recent dealings.

Their discussions were passionate and intense, ranging from keeping tabs on Leonora's movements to gathering intelligence on her new associates. Despite the various backgrounds and perspectives, the alliance was united by a common purpose: to safeguard the family legacy.

As their strategies began to take shape, Liliana felt a renewed sense of hope. However, she knew that for their efforts to truly succeed, they would need Giovanni's support. With his intellect and insight, he could be a formidable ally.

One evening, after the group had dispersed, Liliana sought out Giovanni. She found him in his chambers, the lute now silent, a reflection of his own quiet contemplation. Taking a deep breath, she began to detail the formation of the alliance and their plans.

Giovanni listened intently, his face a mixture of surprise, admiration, and pain. "You've done all this?" he whispered, eyes glistening.

Liliana nodded, "We need you, Giovanni. Now more than ever."

He looked at her, the weight of recent events still evident

in his eyes, but there was also a flicker of determination. "If it means saving our family, and ensuring that Matteo's death was not in vain," he began, voice faltering, "then you have my sword and my heart."

Liliana smiled gently, embracing her brother. The path ahead was treacherous, but with Giovanni by her side and a loyal alliance to support them, she felt a glimmer of hope.

****

Liliana stood on her balcony, overlooking the city. The sprawling landscape was illuminated by the soft glow of lanterns, a city alive with dreams, ambitions, and secrets. Her thoughts raced, reflecting on the recent events and what they meant for the family legacy. The wind gently tugged at her hair and whispered promises of challenges yet to come. And as the moon hung high, casting its silvery glow upon her, she made a silent pledge to herself and to the generations of Morosinis past. No matter the cost, she would protect their name, their honour, and their future. Her determination was unyielding, as sturdy as the ancient stones that built their great city.

Later that evening, an ornate envelop bearing the seal of Master Elric arrived. It was addressed to Liliana.

Dearest Liliana,

I fear for the Morosini family. My studies have led me to a concerning discovery about the sapphire. It is not merely a gem that amplifies ambition, but a cursed relic bound to an ancient entity. This entity feeds on power and desire, and if allowed, will take full possession of its host. Your mother may already be under its influence, more than we initially believed.

To break its hold, the gem must be cleansed in the waters of San Giorgio Maggiore's sacred well at dawn, during the first light of the new moon. But be wary, for the sapphire will resist and the entity may use its host to prevent its own weakening.

May the winds guide your path,
Master Elric

However, Liliana didn't know that the letter had even arrived, her mother had intercepted it first. As Leonora sat in her chamber, the latter lay opened on her desk. Candles flickered, casting shadows that danced on the walls. Her fingers traced the words penned by Master Elric. A bitter taste filled her mouth. Her own children, plotting against her. But this wasn't a sign of betrayal; to her, it was a sign of weakness. The Morosini legacy would rise to unmatched greatness, and she would ensure it, even if it meant casting aside those she once held dear.

The silent rage building within her was tangible. Plots and schemes began to form in her mind. As Leonora held the letter over a nearby candle, igniting it, her eyes, cold and calculating, reflected the firelight, promising a storm on the horizon. The game had changed, and she was prepared to make her move.

Chapter 10

The palatial Morosini estate had witnessed countless crucial moments in Venice's storied history, but the present gathering in its opulent reception hall was an affair few would have ever envisioned. Two families, whose blood feud was the stuff of Venetian legends, were now seated across from each other, their ancestors' fierce battles replaced by the subtle warfare of polite conversation and veiled negotiations.

Leonora, in a dress of deep green that shimmered under the glow of the chandeliers, sat with a straight back, every inch the matriarch of the Morosini family. Opposite her were the Grimaldis - a family that once revealed in the misfortunes of the Morosinis. Their patriarch, Count Marco Grimaldi, was a man of advancing years, his once-black hair now a shade of distinguished gray. Beside him sat his cunning and graceful daughter, Donatella.

To the casual observer, the gathering might have seemed like a reunion of old friends. There was laughter, glasses raised in toasts, and tales of yore shared. However, every gesture, every smile, every seemingly benign remark was loaded with meaning. These two families knew each other's history by heart, and though they appeared to be engaging in amiable conversation, they were in fact engaged in a high-stakes dance of diplomacy.

As plates of delicacies were passed around, the talk veered towards the shared interests of the two families.

Venice had always been a nexus of power, trade, and intrigue. Both families had, at various points in history, aimed for the same goals, and more often than not, crossed swords in their quests. But times had changed. Leonora, with her shrewd business acumen and political might, had reshaped the landscape of Venetian power structures. And now, the Grimaldis sought alignment.

Count Marco, clearing his throat, began, "Lady Leonora, it is no secret that our families have… a complex history. But we believe in looking to the future. Venice's prosperity lies in unity, in collaborative strength. It's time the Grimaldis and the Morosinis stood together."

Leonora, pausing to take a sip from her wine, responded, "I am glad to hear that. The past is a tapestry of lessons, and it's up to us to interpret them wisely for the future. Tell me, Count Marco, what do you propose?"

The Count, leaning forward with anticipation, detailed their proposal. It was an ambitious plan that involved shared trade routes, pooling resources, and setting up join ventures in uncharted territories. The Grimaldis had vast networks but lacked the Morosini wealth, while Leonora had both the capital and the ambition to expand but needed the Grimaldi connections to ensure smooth operations.

The evening wore on, with detailed discussions, clarifications, and negotiations. The weight of the moment was tangible. Here were two families, with a bloodied history, on the cusp of forging an alliance that could reshape Venice's future.

As the clock tower tolled midnight, an agreement was reached. Documents were fetched, scribed, and stamped.

Leonora and Count Marco shook hands, sealing the pact with the gravity it deserved. The ancestral lands that have been part of the Morosini heritage since the dawn of time, now belonged to the Grimaldis - everything except for the Palazzo. And with access to the Grimaldi's vast influential networks, the Morosini name would be lifted ever higher.

As the Grimaldis departed, the Morosini estate was abuzz. Some family members were ecstatic about the potential benefits of this new alliance. Others, deeply rooted in the past, were skeptical, even horrified at the idea of trusting the Grimaldis.

But in her chamber, Leonora sat reflecting. She had taken a gamble, but it was a calculated one. The Grimaldis, for all their past betrayals, were now in a position where they needed the Morosini support. Leonora had ensured that the terms were heavily in her favour. She had turned a historic enmity into an advantageous partnership, further cementing her position as a force to be reckoned with.

Yet, in the quiet solitude of her room, she couldn't help but ponder. Had she pushed too far, too fast? Only time would tell.

As days turned into weeks, whispers filled the air of Venice. They weren't the awed murmurs that accompanied the Morosinis in times of yore, but rather, hushed conversations of apprehension and unease. Words like 'domination', 'unyielding', and 'merciless' were frequently associated with Lady Leonora. The alliance with the Grimaldis, which many had initially seen as a masterstroke, now served as evidence of her unrelenting ambition.

While the streets were vibrant and the markets thrived, a

shadow seemed to have descended upon the city's elite. Merchant families, smaller clans, and even some members of the Council began to view Leonora with a mix of fear and respect. She had achieved the formidable task of subduing the Grimaldis, a family renowned for their cunning and treachery. If she could do that, what hope did any of them have if they found themselves in her crosshairs?

At private gatherings and soirees, the Morosini name was spoken with an air of caution. Some remembered the family as guardians of Venetian tradition and champions of its prosperity. But now, Leonora's rapid ascent had transformed that perception. While none could question her dedication to Venice's welfare, the means by which she sought that end were becoming increasingly controversial.

One particular merchant, who ran several textile enterprises, shared with his confidantes, "Leonora's tactics are not just aggressive, they're relentless. She squeezed the Grimaldis till they had no choice. One by one, she's ensuring that no one remains who could challenge her."

In the piazzas and wine houses, tales of traders who tried to oppose Leonora's terms and were subsequently ruined spread like wildfire. Many believed she had informants everywhere, collecting tidbits of information, which she then used to her advantage. Those who once stood tall in the halls of power now hesitated to even voice a whisper of dissent against her.

This climate of fear and respect was exactly what Leonora had been working toward. It ensured her endeavours went unchallenged and her decisions uncontested. However, there was an undercurrent of unrest.

Small factions began discussing the possibility of forming a coalition strong enough to counter her influence. The question was whether they could ever truly unite, given the apprehension that Leonora's network of informants might expose their plans.

But for now, Leonora's grip on Venice was unyielding. As she gazed from her balcony, the canals and architecture of the city laid out below her, she felt invincible. She was shaping a legacy that would be remembered for ages to come. Her vision for the Morosini family, and for Venice itself, was becoming a reality. The costs and the methods, in her mind, were justifiable for the grandeur of the endgame.

Still, in the solitude of her chambers, in the quiet moments before sleep claimed her, doubts did occasionally creep in. The weight of her actions, the lives affected, the legacy she was crafting - were they truly for the betterment of Venice, or had personal ambition blurred the lines? As these thoughts raced through her mind, a plan began to form, one that would further cement her influence within Venice's upper echelons.

Marriage, after all, had always been a tool of power and alliance for the Venetian nobility. And Leonora, with her keen political acumen, recognised the opportunity before her. A distant cousin of the Morosini family, young Isabella, was of marriageable age. A girl of beauty and wit, she had often been overlooked in the larger family dynamics. However, in Leonora's mind, she was the perfect piece in the intricate chess game of Venetian politics.

Leonora called upon her vast network of contacts, seeking out the most beneficial marriage prospects for

Isabella. Several names were brought forth, but one stood out amongst them - Lord Francesco of the Dandolo family. The Dandolos, while not as prominent as the Morosinis or Grimaldis, were steadily rising in influence. An alliance with them would not only bring substantial dowries but also open doors to previously unexplored avenues of power and commerce.

With determination in her step, Leonora invited Lord Dandolo and his family to the Morosini estate. The mansion was abuzz with anticipation as the best chefs were called upon to prepare a feast, and musicians practiced their harmonies to perfection.

As the Dandolos arrived, they were visibly taken aback by the grandeur on display. Lord Dandolo, a tall man with sharp features and a carefully groomed beard, looked around appreciatively. The initial pleasantries exchanged were filled with mutual admiration and veiled curiosity.

Throughout the evening, Leonora masterfully steered the conversation towards the potential union between Isabella and Francesco. The advantages of such a union were subtly hinted at, the shared prosperity and combined power the two families would wield in the heart of Venice.

Lord Dandolo, being no novice to politics himself, recognised the benefits but played his cards close to his chest. However, as the evening progressed, the mutual understanding became evident. By the time dessert was served, a subtle nod between Lord Dandolo and Leonora signalled that an agreement was in the making.

Isabella, for her part was a mixture of nerves and excitement. Francesco, with his refined manners and intelligent conversation, was intriguing. The prospect of being a bridge between two great families, while daunting, also offered a sense of purpose.

As the evening drew to a close and the guests departed, the Morosini estate once again settled into its nocturnal calm. But inside, the wheels of politics and power continued to turn. Leonora, having successfully brokered a potential alliance, felt a renewed sense of control. The intricate tapestry of Venice's power dynamics was reshaping, and she was the one pulling the threads. However, with her rising dominance came whispers, murmurs that dared to question her actions, motives, and methods.

It began subtly. Political opponents would speak out against her, critiquing her dealings with the Grimaldis, her unabashed ambition. But these voices of opposition did not last. One by one, they began to vanish. It wasn't a loud process; it was done in hushed tones, quiet disappearances in the night. Some said they left Venice to escape her gasp. Others whispered that the depths of the Venetian canals held more secrets than anyone knew.

Master Elric, with his vast knowledge and connections, became a vocal critic. Having served Venice with his scholarly pursuits, he was a respected figure in both academic and noble circles. The venerable scholar, who once helped Liliana and Giovanni, was deeply troubled by the path the Morosini matriarch tread. He penned op-eds, openly questioning her tactics, calling for unity and ethics in leadership.

That, combined with the recent arrival of his letter regarding the sapphire, did not sit well with Leonora. Master

Elric was more than a mere critic; he was a thorn in her side, a voice that could not be easily drowned, and a crazy one at that. All this talk of demons and curses, it's surprising Elric was ever able to attain such a high status in the throes of the scholarly elite, and he should be gotten rid of. One evening, after an especially passionate public critique, Master Elric failed to return home. His chambers, filled with scrolls and manuscripts, remained silent, his inkwell left undisturbed.

The news of his disappearance sent shockwaves throughout Venice. But no one felt it more than Liliana and Giovanni. For them, Master Elric was more than just a mentor; he was a beacon of hope, a voice of reason amidst the chaos that was their family's dynamics. Liliana's heart sank as she remembered their last conversation, his sage advice. Giovanni, still reeling from his own grief, felt another layer of despair envelope him.

Rumours and speculations spread like wildfire. While no evidence pointed directly to Leonora, those in the inner circles knew better. The message was clear: oppose Leonora, and you face the direst of consequences.

Liliana and Giovanni, in their grief and anger, were conflicted. Their mother, the woman who gave them life, was now a force of destruction, leaving a trail of devastation in her wake. They clung to each other, seeking solace, trying to comprehend the depth of the abyss their family had plunged into.

Leonora, meanwhile, continued her scent, seemingly untouched by the murmurs around her. Her grip on Venice tightened, and those who once dared to voice their concerns now thought better of it. The mighty Venetian sunsets cast long shadows, but none darker than the one Leonora now cast over the city she aimed to control completely.

Night after night, as darkness wrapped Venice in its embrace, the once lively streets turned into murmuring alleyways, where every corner held whispered conversations. Fear permeated the very essence of the city, creating an atmosphere of distrust and unease.

In the many taverns and inns scattered throughout the districts, tales of woe and suspicions began to flourish. Hushed voices spoke of masked figures donning ornamental ravens, seen standing outside the homes of critics and rivals the night before they disappeared. Whispers in the markets told of boats, shrouded in darkness, moving silently through the canals, avoiding the main waterways, their purposes unclear but sinister. The word "Morosini" became synonymous with dread, and many Bega to make the sign of protection when it was uttered.

These were not just baseless rumours. There were too many instances, too many patterns. The once proud noble families, who openly discussed politics and strategies, now refrained from voicing their opinions, especially if they differed from Leonora's. The most telling signs were the silences - the gaps where once-prominent voices had been, now eerily quiet.

An old washerwoman, known for her tales and rumours, told of a night when she'd seen cloaked figures entering the Morosini estate, their hands stained as if with fresh ink or perhaps something more sinister. A fisherman spoke of strange, heavy weights he'd pulled up in his net near the Morosini waters, dropping them hastily back for fear of what they might contain. A bard, usually singing praises of nobility, subtly shifted his tunes to mournful ballads of lost souls and a city in chains.

In the midst of all these rumours, two figures stood out - Liliana and Giovanni. To the public eye, they remained the grieving children of a powerful matriarch, but behind closed doors, they wrestled with their mother's legacy and the burden it placed upon them. It was clear to them that these weren't mere stories; they were cries for help, for justice. Yet, confronting their mother directly would be dangerous, even for them.

As the days turned into weeks, the weight of the whispers grew too large to ignore. Anonymous letters began to appear at churches, city squares, and even within the homes of some nobility. These letters spoke of the dark dealings of Leonora Morosini, urging the citizens of Venice to rise against the threat looming over them. Some dismissed these as the work of political rivals, while others saw them as the desperate please of a city under siege.

****

In the deepest recesses of the Morosini estate, behind walls adorned with tapestries and art, lay hidden chambers that held the secrets of generations. And it was in one of these chambers, a room that had been locked for as long as Liliana could remember, that she stumbled upon her mother's carefully guarded secrets.

The chamber was dimly lit, a single window high up on the wall providing just enough light to make out the contours of furniture below. Dust motes danced in the thin beam of sunlight. Heavy drapes, once vibrant but now faded with time, lined the walls. And there, in the centre, was an ornate desk, littered with scrolls, ledgers, and quills.

Approaching cautiously, Liliana opened one of the ledgers, her fingers brushing against the rough texture of the pages. The neat, tight script that filled them revealed financial transactions - vast sums of money being transferred between accounts, payments made to names she recognised as prominent families, and coded entries hinting at more sinister exchanges.

As she leafed through the ledgers, a pattern emerged. Payments marked as 'gifts' or 'donations' coincided with political decisions that favoured the Morosini family. There were names of officials who had suddenly changed their stance of policies, notes beside their names that read 'persuaded', or 'ensured loyalty'. It was clear these weren't mere business transactions; they were tools of control, wielded with precision by Leonora.

One record, in particular, stood out. A series of payments to the Grimaldis, each one tied to a date that marked a betrayal against the Morosinis. The realisation hit Liliana like a ton of bricks. Her mother wasn't just making alliances; she was buying loyalty, ensuring that no knife would ever be poised at their backs again.

Hastily, she scribbled copies of the most incriminating pages, concealing them within her attire. She knew she had to act swiftly, for if Leonora found out she had been in this chamber, there would be dire consequences.

That very night, under the cloak of darkness, Liliana

called a clandestine meeting with her trusted allies. In a secluded corner of a dimly lit tavern, she unfurled the pages, laying them out on the wooden table. The faces of those present turned from confusion to shock and then to understanding. Each page told a tale of manipulation, bribery, and deceit.

The group began to discuss strategies. They realised that while the ledgers were powerful proof, they would need more evidence to counteract Leonora's tightening grip on Venice. Promising to reconvene with a plan, they dispersed, slipping away into the shadows, determined to unravel the web Leonora had so carefully woven around the city.

****

The halls of the Morosini estate echoed with the sound of hurried footsteps and hushed whispers, as servants scurried about, preparing for a grand announcement. Heavy crimson drapes were drawn back, allowing the sun to spill into the marbled atrium. Tall, ornate candelabras flickered, casting a soft glow on the intricate mosaic floor. At the head of the room stood Leonora, her regal attire making her appear larger than life, and accented by the sapphire that hung around her neck.

Liliana, having just returned from her meeting, was unaware of the commotion until she stepped into the main hall. She felt the weight of many eyes upon her, making her uneasy.

With a sweeping gesture, Leonora commanded the room's attention. "It gives me great pleasure to announce," she began, her voice resonating with authority, "the engagement of our beloved daughter, Liliana to the esteemed Duke Alarico of Verona!"

A gasp swept through the room. Glasses clinked, congratulatory murmurs arose, and an orchestra began to play a celebratory tune. All eyes turned ti Liliana, searching for a reaction.

She felt as though the ground had been yanked from beneath her feet. Duke Alarico was known for his vast lands and unmatched political influence, but he was also known for his ruthlessness and ambition. The match would indeed be a powerful one, securing the Morosinis in an unassailable position. But for Liliana, it was a shackle.

Attempting to keep her composure, she curtsied politely, even managing a week smile. But inside, a tempest raged.

After the initial shock subsided and the assembly began to indulge in festivities, Liliana pulled her mother aside, her eyes searching for some hint of compassion. "Mother, why was I not informed of this? I have no desire to be wed to the duke!"

Leonora's gaze was as cold as the marble statues that lined their home. "This is bigger than your desires, child," she replied icily. "This is about our family, our legacy. Your feelings are a small price to pay."

Liliana's plea, the desperation evident in her eyes, went unnoticed by her mother, who was already entertaining congratulatory guest.

The news traveled fast, reaching every corner of Venice by the next dawn. The streets buzzed with talk of the upcoming nuptials, of the alliance that would reshape the political landscape. The Morosini household was no different, with tension in every whispered conversation, every sidelong glance.

****

Under the dim, flickering light of the secret chamber where they met, tension crackled in the air as members of Liliana's alliance gathered. One seat remained conspicuously empty, its usual occupant nowhere to be seen. Glances were exchanged, questions silently asked and answered without a word spoken.

It was no secret that Lorenzo had shown signs of unease in their last gathering, his gaze darting nervously, sweat beading on his brow. The alliance had always been built on trust, but the stakes were now undeniably high. Fear was a dangerous contagion that could spread if not contained.

Ripples of unease flowed through the group. Whispers and hushed conversations broke out as they speculated on the reasons for Lorenzo's abrupt departure. Was it mere fear, or was there something more sinister at play?

Evidence soon emerged, adding fuel to their fears. Documents, previously accessibly only to the alliance, were discovered in unexpected places, hinting at the possibility of a traitor in their midst. The very strategies they had meticulously crafted were now potentially exposed, leaving them vulnerable to Leonora's machinations.

It became evident to the alliance that every moment of inaction only served to empower Leonora further. Their secrecy had been their shield, but with potential cracks emerging, they needed to fortify their defences and act. They began devising new plans, anticipating Leonora's moves, and preparing to counteract. The clock was ticking as they raced against time to ensure their efforts weren't in vain.

****

Golden rays of twilight faded into the blue depths of the Venetian evening as Leonora sat in her private chambers, a glass of rich wine in hand. The room was a testament to her power, but her contemplation of that legacy was interrupted by the soft sound of parchment sliding under the door. With a furrowed brow, she reached down, unfurling the missive to reveal a warning scribbled in hurried handwriting.

Her eyes scanned the words, each line making her grip on the glass tighter, the red liquid within threatening to spill over. Someone, somewhere knew about her children's secret gatherings. The very thought, the audacity of them plotting possibly against her, was a burning brand against her pride.

For a moment, anger clouded her vision. But Leonora was nothing if not calculated. With renewed purpose, she descended into the corridors beneath the Morosini estate. Past dungeons and forgotten storage rooms, she navigated with familiarity until she reached a heavy wooden door, guarded by symbols and incantations that whispered of old magics.

The door groaned open, revealing an underground chamber illuminated by an eerie blue glow. In its centre stood a figure draped in dark robes, their face obscured by the shadow of a hood. Leonora approached, her footsteps echoing on the stone floor, each step a testament to her unwavering resolve.

The mysterious figure, sensing her arrival, turned to face her. Their exchange was silent, a communion of gestures and subtle movements. It was evident that this was not their first meeting, their shared history evident in the unspoken understanding between them. The figure presented Leonora with an object, its nature unclear, but its significance astounding.

With her consultation complete, Leonora emerged from the depths, her resolve hardened like tempered steel. She returned to her chamber, the very heart of her power, and approached the grand window that framed the Venetian skyline.

As the city lights shimmered below, Leonora's gaze was drawn to a particular item on her desk. The sapphire heirloom. The genesis of her ascent to unmatched power. The gem seemed to pulse, its inner light dancing in tandem with her heartbeat. The reached out, letting her fingers graze its surface, feeling its cool allure.

"To challenge the Morosini reign, *my* reign," she whispered to herself, her voice filled with an icy determination, "is to challenge fate itself."

With the city sprawling before her, Leonora's fingers tenderly closed around the sapphire heirloom. Slowly, almost ceremoniously, she clasped it around her neck. The gem pulsed against her skin, its allure undeniable. In the ambient light, the sapphire gleamed menacingly, echoing the dangerous gleam in Leonora's eyes.

Chapter 11

The water of the canal reflected the pale light of the waning moon, the ripples dancing with the gentle caress of the Venetian night breeze. From afar, one might think Venice was in a tranquil slumber, but the waterways told a different story. A ship, larger than the common vessels that navigated these channels, approached slowly and cautiously. Its masts were dark silhouettes against the shimmering night sky, its oars gliding smoothly, barely causing a splash.

At the helm stood a figure. Though shadows concealed most of his features, there was an undeniable aura of authority about him, a certainty in every step he took on the deck, even as he chose to remain hidden in the cloak of darkness. The ship itself was a magnificent sight to behold, bearing foreign craftsmanship and intricate designs.

Mooring at a secluded dock, the ship's crew moved with practiced precision. They worked in silence, communicating with mere gestures and nods, understanding the gravity of discretion this moment demanded. The night was their ally, and they intended to keep it that way. They swiftly began to unload crates, all marked with the same distinguished insignia: a silver bell.

From the ship's stern, the cloaked figure observed the proceedings. He didn't participate but was deeply involved in every movement, every decision. From the way he tilted his head to catch faint sounds to the manner in which his fingers occasionally brushed the hilt of a concealed blade, it was evident that this return was neither casual nor without risks.

As the crew made their preparations, a smaller boat detached from the ship. Two men rowed, their oars moving in tandem, while the cloaked figure took a seat, his silhouette still the most dominating presence. The boat made its way deeper into the heart of Venice, the looming structures on either side a testament to the city's history.

The cloaked man's journey was uneventful, yet tension hung in the air. It was clear that he knew these waters, these alleyways, and these buildings. Venice was not unfamiliar territory, but the city he once knew had changed, its heartbeat altered by new allegiances and simmering tensions. As the boat navigated the winding waterways, one could almost sense a quiet dread settling over Venice, as if the city sensed the return of an old spectre.

Finally, the boat reached its destination - a quiet, abandoned palazzo, its facade revealing nothing of its interiors. With a soft thud, the boat came to a halt, and he stepped onto the stone steps leading to the mansion. There was a slight pause, a moment of stillness, before the figure opened the doors, revealing a dimly lit corridor.

The figure stepped in, and as the doors closed behind him, the silver bell insignia, now left behind on the ship and the crates, seemed to resonate louder than ever.

The palazzo, though abandoned, was an architectural marvel. Tall, arched windows lined the exterior, now covered in a thick layer of grime, hiding the interior from prying eyes. The entrance hall was grand, with a once-gilded ceiling that now showed signs of decay and neglect.

Cobwebs hung like intricate lace, testifying to the years of desolation.

But Antonio saw beyond the decay. Each room, each corridor, held potential. He quickly assigned tasks to his men, who had started ferrying in the crates from the boat. The place needed to be fortified, secured. The larger halls on the ground floor were designated as storage and meeting areas. They quickly got to work, unboxing provisions, weapons, maps, and other essentials, setting up a makeshift armoury and planning room.

As the hours went by, what once stood as a relic of the past started taking on a new life. Rooms were cleaned out, old furniture repaired or replaced, and security measures discreetly installed. The palazzo's grand ballroom, with its sprawling space and tall columns, was transformed into a war room of sorts. A large wooden table was placed in the centre, surrounded by chairs. On the table, a map of Venice was spread out, held down by small weights on each corner. Adjacent chambers were repurposed as living quarters and infirmaries, equipped with beds, medical supplies, and other amenities.

The underground cellars, cool and damp, became storage for more sensitive items. They were naturally defensible, with thick walls and a maze-like layout. Here, Antonio's most trusted lieutenants cataloged the incoming shipments - barrels of gunpowder, racks of weaponry, and crates of preserved food and fresh water. With the city's complex political landscape, it was imperative they be prepared for any eventuality.

On the palazzo's rooftop, a small team worked diligently

to set up a discreet signalling system using lanterns and coded messages. It overlooked much of the city, and with the right equipment, could serve as both a lookout point and a means of covert communication.

By dawn, the transformation was remarkable. The palazzo, once a silent testament to time's ravages, now hummed with restrained energy. The air was thick with purpose, with Antonio at the centre, orchestrating each move, each decision. Each room of the refurbished palazzo seemed to pulse with life, a stark contrast to the desolation that had once held sway. But for all its renewed vibrancy, the true machinations of the palazzo remained shrouded in mystery to the outside world.

In the heart of this hive, Antonio assembled a group of trusted individuals. These were not the brawny labourers who had fortified the palazzo but rather individuals with a different skill set: the art of espionage. They were his eyes and ears in Venice, individuals who could blend into crowds, listen to whispers in the marketplaces, and frequent the taverns without drawing attention.

With a map of Venice spread out in front of him, Antonio meticulously began detailing assignments. One was tasked with tracking Leonora's movements, learning of her daily routines, allies, and places she frequented. Another was given the duty of gauging the sentiments within the Morosini household - the alliances, the fractures, and the mood of its members. And finally, one agent was singularly focused on the whereabouts of the sapphire heirloom, the glittering centrepiece of Antonio's long-held ambitions.

These spies, outfitted with disguises and false identities,

melted into the city's streets, using its canals, rooftops, and alleyways to their advantage. They operated in the shadows, always watching, always listening, documenting everything in coded scripts that only Antonio and a few others could decipher.

Weeks turned into months, and the information began pouring in. Pigeons bearing coded messages would frequently land on the palazzo's rooftops, each note more enlightening than the last. Patterns emerged - Leonora's increasing visits to an underground chamber, the restlessness within the Morosini household, and, most crucially, whispers about the sapphire heirloom being moved to a new, undisclosed location.

Antonio meticulously recorded each piece of intelligence, piecing together a puzzle that would guide his next moves. He knew the importance of patience and precision. Any false move or hastily made decision could jeopardise his meticulously laid plans. With that thought firmly anchored in his mind, Antonio took measured steps to engage with certain individuals within the city's intricate web of power and influence.

Away from the main streets and popular canals lay hidden corners where old debts and loyalties still held sway. These shadowed enclaves and unassuming taverns played host to an underground network, where grievances against Leonora and the current state of affairs found a voice.

Being a merchant of repute, Antonio had left an indelible mark on Venice's socio-economic landscape. Many of those he had dealt with in the past had seen their influence wane under Leonora's tightening grip. Their businesses had suffered, their prominence had diminished, and their silent resentment had grown.

With discreet rendezvous orchestrated under moonlit skies, Antonio met with these individuals. There was the cloth trader whose imports had been heavily taxed since Leonora's ascendancy. There was the shipbuilder, once a favoured contractor for the Morosini family, who now found himself sidelined in favour of foreign businesses. And there was the mask-maker, an artist of great renown, who felt stifled by Leonora's new regulations on public events and festivals.

Each of these meetings, carefully planned to avoid any suspicion, had a singular purpose: to gauge the level of dissent and to cultivate an alliance against a common adversary. Antonio, with his intimate knowledge of the city's political and business underpinnings, knew just which strings to pull, which grievances to highlight, and which promises to make. It was as if he had a map of Venice not in terms of canals and buildings, but in connections, vulnerabilities, and ambitions. Each step was calculated, each move precise, ensuring that he played to the strengths and weaknesses of the city's power players.

Antonio frequented establishments that once knew his patronage well. In the dim glow of lantern-lit taverns, he discreetly rekindled alliances, making use of the trust and rapport he had built over the years. Each of these connections offered him an avenue, a thread to tun on, to weave a larger tapestry of opposition against Leonora's reign. The deeper he delved, the clearer it became: not everyone within Leonora's circle remained fiercely loyal to her cause. Some were beginning to see the cracks, the signs of overreach and ruthlessness that seemed more about personal power than the welfare of the city. And among them was a man whose loyalty to the Morosini family was once beyond question - Lorenzo.

The streets of the city whispered tales of Lorenzo's discontent. It was said that he had grown disillusioned, watching the woman he had sworn to protect, transform into a figure he hardly recognised. For a guard of his caliber, duty and honour held great significance, and witnessing the depths Leonora was willing to sink to secure her power, left a bitter taste.

Antonio saw in Lorenzo's disquiet a valuable asset. He sent intermediaries, men he trusted implicitly, to approach Lorenzo. Through hushed conversations in secluded alleyways and discreet exchanges in shadowed corners, the bond began to form. They spoke of a Venice that thrived on unity, on shared ambition, and not on the fears of its citizens. Antonio made it clear that his intentions were not just about personal vendetta but a genuine concern for the city he loved.

Meanwhile, Antonio expanded his influence, reaching out to magistrates, bureaucrats, and even a few influential merchants who had felt the sting of Leonora's strategies. Bribes were offered, favours exchanged, and promises made. With each passing day, the network of those willing to oppose Leonora grew, bolstered by the assurance that they weren't standing alone.

However, securing Lorenzo's allegiance was the crowning achievement. As someone so intimately woven into Leonora's inner circle, his support offered insights, access, and symbolic victory for Antonio. A clear message that even those closest to Leonora could see the storm on the horizon.

The depths of Leonora's obsession with the sapphire was no secret to Antonio, but the recent intelligence he received from his spies painted a vivid image of the extent to which Leonora had gone.

In the grand halls of the Morosini residence, the guards had doubled. New faces, armoured and stern, patrolled the corridors with an almost mechanical precision. Entry points, once open for the high society of Venice, were now scrutinised, every guest passing through an exhaustive series of checks. The whispers of the courtiers spoke of a heightened paranoia, a shadow of anxiety that seemed to permeate the very walls. Leonora's chambers, once a place of respite and reflection, now appeared as a fortified sanctum, heavily guarded with only a select few allowed entrance.

The sapphire itself had become an almost constant presence by her side. Gone were the days when it was merely an ornamental piece to be worn at grand occasions. Leonora was seen clutching it, sometimes absentmindedly caressing its surface as if drawing strength from its lustrous depths. It was whispered that she had even taken to sleeping with it, placed securely under her pillow, a talisman against the dangers of the night.

Antonio surmised that the gem's influence was growing, tightening its grip on Leonora's psyche. This presented both a challenge and an opportunity. On one hand, infiltrating the inner sanctum of the Morosini estate had become a daunting task, fraught with the risk of exposure. But on the other, Leonora's increasing dependency on the heirloom signalled a potential vulnerability, an Achilles' heel that could be exploited.

Given the intensified security, Antonio knew that a direct approach would be foolish. He would need to be patient, meticulous in his planning. The fortified walls of the Morosini residence, the increased patrols, and the heightened scrutiny were all clear indicators of Leonora's paranoia and readiness. The very environment screamed of her anticipation of a direct assault, almost as if she was beckoning her adversaries to challenge her in her fortress.

As Antonio reviewed the intelligence from his spies and mulled over his strategies, he began to grasp the magnitude of his task. A direct confrontation would not only be dangerous but also might solidify Leonora's hold on power. If she could defeat an open challenge, her reign would be legitimised in the eyes of many, and her detractors would be silenced, potentially for good.

But Antonio was not one to be easily deterred. Instead of a frontal assault, perhaps a subtler approach was needed, one that would destabilise Leonora from within, making her question her own decisions and the loyalty of those around her.

Planting seeds of doubt within her inner circle would be a good start. If Antonio could manipulate the narrative, turn her most trusted allies into potential threats in her eyes, it could create cracks in her arbor. With Lorenzo already showing signs of wavering loyalty, he might be the perfect piece to move in this intricate game of chess.

Furthermore, if the city's key figures began to openly express their doubts about Leonora, it could sway public opinion. Venice was a city of merchants, traders, and artists, all of whom depended on stability and predictability. If Leonora's rule was perceived as erratic or dangerous for the city's prosperity, it could turn the tide against her.

While the sapphire was a powerful tool in Leonora's arsenal, it was also her potential downfall. Its allure, its magnetic pull, its magic, was something Antonio could exploit. By fuelling rumours about its true nature, its potential dangers, and its mysterious origins, he could make it a source of fear and intrigue. Even the most fortified of fortresses had its weaknesses, and for Leonora, the allure of the heirloom could potentially be her downfall.

As Antonio gathered his inner circle in the refurbished halls of the palazzo, an air of anticipation permeated the room. Maps of the city, blueprints of the Morosini residence, and detailed reports of Leonora's daily routines were spread out on a large wooden table, illuminated by the soft glow of candles. The room was filled with Venice's most cunning minds, all united by a singular objective.

For hours they deliberated, weighing the risks and rewards of each approach. Every entrance, every guard post, every secret passageway was considered. But with Leonora's intensified security and her near-obsessive proximity to the sapphire, a simple theft was out of the question.

"It's not just about taking the heirloom," Antonio began, his voice echoing a depth of experience. "It's about ensuring its theft weakens her grip on power, without alerting her to our true intentions."

The two-pronged approach emerged from these deliberations. First, a distraction - something grand and undeniable that would draw Leonora's attention, and more importantly, her guards and security away from the residence. With the city's key figures now voicing their dissent, perhaps a public demonstration, a protest against her rule, would be the perfect ploy. It would not only capitalise on the growing unrest but would force Leonora to deploy her forces to maintain order.

With the city's eyes turned to this demonstration, the second prong, stealth, would come into play. A small, elite team would infiltrate the Morosini residence, using the chaos outside as cover. Their objective was singular: retrieve the sapphire heirloom without detection.

The plan was intricate, layered with potential pitfalls and uncertainties. But if executed flawlessly, it promised not only the retrieval of the sapphire but also a significant blow to Leonora's reputation and hold over Venice.

****

The grand halls of the abandoned palazzo echoed with the clatter of steel against steel. Day after day, under the dim light filtering through the aged, stained windows, Antonio drilled his allies in combat. These were not mere sparring sessions; they were intense, rigorous, and designed to ensure each participant was battle-ready. Some of these men and women were seasoned fighters, while others had only known the roughness of street brawls. All were now unified under Antonio's banner, learning, adapting, and preparing for what lay ahead.

Antonio himself led the training, his years as a merchant not having dulled his skill with the blade. With sift, precise movements, he parried, attacked, and demonstrated techniques that would be vital in their upcoming confrontations. He pushed them hard, understanding that the difference between life and death would come down to split-second decisions and reactions.

In the evenings, after the clashing of swords had ceased and a hush descended upon the palazzo, Antonio could be found poring over maps of the city, studying potential choke points, guard rotations, and escape routes. It was evident to all who observed him that he was driven by something more profound than mere strategy or ambition.

His eyes, once lively with the energy of commerce and trade, now carried a determined glint, reflecting a fire fuelled by betrayal and a deep-seated need for vengeance. Antonio had been wronged, and his desire to reclaim his place was unwavering. He envisioned a Venice where the likes of Leonora could not rise unchecked, where power was balanced, and where he could once again walk its streets as a respected figure. This vision was the beacon that guided his every move, every decision, driving him and his allies forward. It was the hope that burned bright in their hearts, even in the darkest moments of their covert operations.

Yet, with every meticulous strategy, every late-night session pouring over maps and details, and each gruelling training, Antonio felt the weight of his mission. The burden of leadership and the magnitude of what he aimed to achieve bore down on him. The weight of decisions that could either reshape Venice's future or see his own downfall was immense. Though the fire of revenge and redemption burned hot within him, the reality of his human limitations began to catch up with him.

One evening, as dusk cast its orange and pink hues over the Venetian skyline, Antonio felt a rare moment of exhaustion, both physical and emotional. He was reminded that, while he was a leader with a mission, he was also a man who had been through profound trials. Realising he needed a brief escape from his consuming purpose, he decided to indulge in a simple pleasure he had long missed: the atmosphere of an authentic Venetian tavern.

Slipping out from his secret base, Antonio, cloaked in shadows and anonymity, meandered through the winding alleys of the city, making his way to a quaint, lesser-known tavern tucked away from the prying eyes of the city's elite. The warm glow of lanterns hung outside its entrance, inviting weary travellers and locals alike.

As he stepped inside, the familiar hum of chatter, laughter, and clinking glasses embraced him. It was a stark contrast to the world he was fighting against outside, a small bubble of normalcy in the midst of chaos. He settled into a quiet corner, ordering a refreshing drink, and for a fleeting moment, allowed himself to just be Antonio Bellini - a man who loved his city and yearned for simpler times. As he took the first sip, the cool liquid rolled down his parched throat, providing immediate solace. Each gulp was an echo of memories past, of days when joy was simpler and ambitions were just dreams waiting to be chased.

The aroma of freshly cooked food wafted from the

kitchen, tickling Antonio's senses. He realised just how much he had missed the taste of a hot, home-cooked Venetian meal. Ordering a plate of his old favourite, *risotto al nero di seppia* - a creamy rice dish stained black with cuttlefish ink and sprinkled with parmesan - Antonio felt a rush of warmth and familiarity as it arrived steaming hot before him.

As he dug into his meal, each bit was a transformative experience. The flavours and textures triggered a cascade of memories, pulling him deeper into the past.

He was back in the prime of his life, surrounded by bustling market streets lined with stalls flaunting silks, spices, and jewellery. Antonio Bellini, the respected merchant, stood tall with a proud glint in his eyes, his silver bell insignia gleaming in the midday sun, representing both his family name and his prosperous business. The canals were alive with song and dance, gondoliers steering their boats with a grace only they possessed, transporting both locals and tourists through the city's waterways. Venice was a city of dreams, and Antonio was it its very heart.

He remembered the evening gatherings at the city squares, where families and friends would come together, share tales of their day, laugh, and rejoice in each other's company. Children would play, while the elderly would exchange stories of their youth. It was a time when Antonio's biggest concern was ensuring the success of his next trade or planning his next voyage.

The weight of power plays, political manoeuvres, and betrayals were unknown to him then. Leonora was just a distant name with ambitions, not the formidable force she had morphed into. Those were the days when sleep came easy, and mornings were greeted with hope and zest.

But as the saying goes, nostalgia has a way of painting pictures rosier than reality. Antonio was engrossed in his memories, the noise of the tavern fading into the background, the taste of his risotto amplifying the vividness of his past.

Suddenly, the past and the present collided. A voice, soft yet unmistakable, broke through his reminiscences. "Antonio?" The voice had a mix of surprise, concern, and a hint of familiarity that sent a chill down his spine. He froze, fork midway to his mouth, as a mix of emotions flooded him - fear, recognition, and an unexpected flutter in his heart. Who in this tavern would or could recognise him?

As Antonio turned around, the dim light of the tavern momentarily shielded the identity of the figure standing before him. But as his eyes adjusted, recognition and disbelief washed over him.

It was Liliana.

Chapter 12

"I thought you left Venice."

There she stood, the woman Antonio was supposed to marry, the woman who was once his heart's desire. Her ebony hair cascaded down her back, the same lustrous locks he once used to admire. Her eyes, however, had changed. They once radiated warmth and love when they looked upon him, but now they held a mix of shock, hurt, and a lingering resentment. The atmosphere in the tavern seemed to thicken; time seemed to slow.

Antonio took a deep breath, the weight of his emotions pressing down on him. "I did," he replied, the edge of vulnerability evident in his voice. "But Venice… it's home. I had to return."

The music and hum of chatter from the other patrons faded to a murmur as the two former lovers navigated the minefield of their shared history. The space between them crackled with a tension that could not be ignored.

Liliana looked away for a moment, as if gathering her thoughts. "Why now, Antonio? After everything that happened?"

He hesitated. "There are many reasons, but primarily, I needed to set things right."

There was a pause, filled only by the ambient sounds of the tavern and the memories of a past they both tried to forget. As the silence grew, it was evident that their feelings for each other were far from gone. The hurt and betrayal might have overshadowed their love temporarily, but now, in close quarters, the undeniable attraction was hard to ignore.

With a soft sigh, Liliana admitted, "Despite it all, I've missed you." The raw honesty of her words took Antonio by surprise.

His throat tightened. "I've missed you too, more than I can express. But I never expected to see you again, especially not here."

Liliana hesitated, biting her lip as she contemplated her next words. "Perhaps it was fate or just plain coincidence. But here we are, and it's clear there's still something between us."

They both knew the implications of their words. Given their current dynamics, any association between them was fraught with danger. Yet, the magnetic pull between them was hard to resist. Liliana's gaze was distant. "We're playing with fire, Antonio. If my mother ever found out-"

"She won't," Antonio interrupted, his voice firm, though there was a hint of doubt in his eyes. "We'll be careful."

"But is it worth it?" she whispered, her voice laden with pain and confusion. "The risks we're taking, the secrets, the lies..."

He reached over, taking her hand in his. The touch sent a shiver up her spine. "Every moment with you is worth it. I regretted every day I spent away from you, every second I wasn't by your side."

Liliana swallowed hard, her eyes shimmering with unshed tears. "I thought I had moved on, bored those feelings. But seeing you, it's as if no time has passed at all.

Yet, everything has changed."

He squeezed her hand reassuringly. "We've both changed, been through so much. But that doesn't mean we can't find our way back to each other."

She withdrew her hand slowly, her fingers lingering on his for a moment longer. "Antonio, my mother has become more ruthless than you can imagine. The things I've seen, the lengths she's gone to maintain power... If she ever learned about us, she'd stop at nothing to keep us apart."

His face darkened, a storm of emotions crossing his features. "I won't let her harm you, Liliana. I promise."

A sad smile tugged at the corners of her lips. "It's not just me I'm worried about. It's you, Antonio. I couldn't bear it if anything happened to you because of our relationship."

He leaned in, his voice gentle but firm. "We'll find a way together. I came back to Venice not just for revenge or to reclaim what was taken from me, but for you. I can't walk away now, not when my heart is telling me to stay."

Liliana looked deep into Antonio's eyes, searching for answers, for reassurance. She found both. With a determined nod, she whispered, "Then let's face this storm together, whatever may come."

Antonio's eyes shone with a determination, but there was also a vulnerability there, one that Liliana had not seen in a long time. The tavern's ambient noise seemed to fade into the background as they both sat there, momentarily lost in their own thoughts. The weight of their decisions, their past, and the impending future pressed heavily on them.

Liliana sighed and rose from her seat. "Come with me," she whispered, beckoning him to follow. They left the tavern discreetly, walking down the narrow streets of Venice. They night had fallen, and the moonlight reflecting off the canals cast an enchanting glow on the city.

She led him to a hidden courtyard, one that they used to frequent when they were courting. A small fountain in the middle trickled gently, its water shimmering under the soft light. Here, away from prying eyes, they could speak freely.

Liliana looked up at Antonio, her face illuminated by the moon's glow. "You must understand, Antonio, that things are not the same. My mother's grip on Venice is tighter than ever. She has eyes and ears everywhere. Our affair could jeopardise not just our lives but those of everyone we hold dear."

Antonio took a step closer, the raw intensity in his gaze making Liliana's heart race. "I understand the dangers, but I also know the depth of our love, Liliana. We can't live in the shadows forever, constantly fearing what might come next."

She hesitated, torn between her duty and her heart. "We need a plan, Antonio. If we're to be together, we need to be smarter than ever. We can't afford any slip-ups."

Antonio moved closer, the proximity stirring old memories and emotions. "I've missed you," he whispered, a raw honesty in his voice. "Every day, every night, I've thought of what we had, and what was taken from us."

Liliana's eyes filled with tears as she took in his words. "I've missed you too," she replied softly. "But things are so complicated now. My mother's influence, the politics... we have to be cautious."

He lifted her chin gently, looking deep into her eyes. "I'm not afraid, Liliana. I've returned to Venice for you, for us.

Whatever challenges lie ahead, we'll face them together."

She smiled weakly, leaning into his embrace. The warmth of his body against hers felt so familiar, so comforting. In that moment, the world outside ceased to exist, and it was just the two of them, wrapped up in their past and the possibility of a future.

Antonio gently brushed a strand of hair behind her ear, and their lips met in a passionate embrace. As they pulled away, he whispered, "I promise, Liliana, no matter what, I'll never let you go again."

They sat down on the stone bench by the fountain, the gentle trickle of water serving as a backdrop to their conversation. They reminisced about the past, their shared dreams and ambitions, the love they had for each other that was interrupted by circumstances.

In the muted glow of the moonlight, every shadow seemed to lean closer, whispering tales of days gone by. Antonio gently cradled Liliana's face, tracing the soft curve of her cheek, as they allowed the silence to speak for them. The lingering scent of jasmine from nearby gardens wafted around them, wrapping them in an intoxicating embrace that mirrored their own. The barriers that once kept them apart seemed to dissolve in that instant. Their lips met, softly at first, then with a fervour that had been simmering for what felt like an eternity.

As their breaths intermingled and their heartbeats synchronised, the world around them seemed to blur. Every sensation, every touch was amplified, a dance of rediscovery. Time seemed suspended, with only the rhythm of the night and the tender warmth they found in each other's arms.

The stars above bore silent witness to their reunion, acting as sentinels to a love that, while tested by trials and tribulations, remained unbroken. Their souls, long yearning for this connection, intertwined in a heated ballet of passion and longing, seeking solace and understanding in the sanctuary they found in each other.

As dawn approached, the reality of their situation started to seep in. Their secret meetings would be risky, but the allure of being together, even for fleeting moments, was too hard to resist. They decided to meet at their old spots, places that held memories, places where they felt safe.

"I'll always find a way to see you," Antonio murmured, taking her hand. "Our love is worth every risk."

Liliana nodded, leaning her head on his shoulder. "I know," she said, her voice filled with emotion. "Just promise me you'll be careful."

"I promise," he replied, sealing their pact with a kiss.

The rising sun painted the sky in hues of gold and orange, marking the beginning of a new day. As they parted, the promise of more stolen moments and the dream of a future together filled their hearts.

****

The clandestine nature of their meetings added a layer of excitement to their rendezvous. The streets, which were once mere pathways, became mazes of longing and anticipation. The alleys whispered secrets, the canals hushed confessions, and every corner held memories of their shared past.

Liliana would leave little notes for Antonio, using coded

language that only they understood, indicating where they should meet next. An inked daisy meant the garden near her ancestral home; a drawn moon meant the terrace overlooking the Grand Canal where they first confessed their love. The rooftops became their sanctuary, the gardens their confession booths. They found seclusion in plain sight, with the city itself aiding their covert trysts.

One evening, they met at the abandoned opera house, a place where they had watched countless performances together. With the grandeur of its prime now faded, it still held the echoes of their younger days. There, under the ornate chandelier that had lost its lustre, they danced to a silent tune, their movements telling tales of longing, reunion, and hope.

Another day, it was the quiet nook by the library where Antonio once read poetry to Liliana, his voice melting into the verses, making her believe every word was written just for her. They revisited those verses, their fingers tracking lines on old parchment, their hearts tracing the timeline of their relationship.

With each stolen moment, their bond strengthened. Their love was like wine aged to perfection, richer and deeper with time. The city, with its secrets and shadows, became their haven, shielding them from prying eyes and gossiping tongues. The streets of the city played an unwitting accomplice to their romance, every bridge and alley bearing witness to their undying love.

But with passion also came the ever-present peril. Every step they took was fraught with danger. The shadows that provided cover could also conceal spies or informants. The weight of their enmity, the city's politics, and Antonio's personal vendetta against Leonora hung like the Sword of Damocles over their heads. They knew the risks, yet the heart yearns for what it desires most, and for Antonio and Liliana, it was each other.

While the vast network of canals and alleys made the city an expert at keeping secrets, every whispered word, every stolen glance had the potential to betray them. There were eyes everywhere, always watching always speculating. A servant might catch a glimpse of them and sell the information to the highest bidder. A rival faction might use their love as a bargaining chip or a weapon against the Morosini family. The stakes were incredibly high.

Antonio had become skilled at navigating Venice's political and social minefields. But this was different. Every time they met, he would sweep the surroundings for any sign of surveillance. They would change their rendezvous points frequently, communicate through coded messages, and even employed trusted individuals to act as lookouts.

Liliana, for her part, became adept at crafting alibis and finding excuses to slip away from her family's prying eyes. She would frequently visit orphanages, under the guise of charity work, or take long walks for fresh air, always ensuring that her trails were covered.

But it wasn't just the external threats that haunted them; the internal turmoil was just as tumultuous. The very foundation of their relationship was built upon the treacherous sands of deception and risk. Liliana often found herself torn between loyalty to her family and her love for Antonio. Nights were the hardest when the weight of their situation would press down on her, and she'd wonder if their love would ever find light beyond the shadows.

Antonio, though resolute in his quest against Leonora, also grappled with guilt. The memory of their broken engagement and the pain it brought Liliana was a wound that never truly healed. He constantly battled the fear that his actions, his very presence, might bring harm to her.

As days turned into weeks, close calls became more frequent. Once, a member of the Morosini household almost spotted Antonio leaving one of their secret spots. Another time, a letter meant for Liliana fell into the wrong hands, and it was only by sheer luck and quick thinking that they managed to retrieve it before its contents were revealed.

One evening, Antonio had sneaked into the Morosini estate's gardens to meet Liliana. Their designated spot was a small alcove, concealed by tall hedges and a statue of Aphrodite. As Antonio waited, he thought he heard soft footsteps approaching from behind. Pressing himself into the shadows, he peeked out and saw a figure approaching.

It was Giovanni.

Antonio's heart raced. He was cornered, the only way out was directly past Giovanni. He watched, frozen, as Giovanni stopped near the statue, seemingly lost in thought. Antonio realised he had left a pendant, a gift for Liliana, on the bench in the alcove, just inches away from Giovanni. If he saw it, he would undoubtedly recognise it, for it bore the emblem of the Bellini family.

The minutes felt like hours. Every rustle of the leaves, every chirp of the night insects seemed amplified. Antonio held his breath, praying Giovanni wouldn't turn his way. He was so close that Antonio could see the faint scars on Giovanni's hand, a remnant of an old duel. He could even smell the familiar scent of the paints and oils and inks that Giovanni so often surrounded himself by.

Suddenly, a distant sound echoed in the courtyard - the laughter of a lady, possible one of Liliana's friends. Giovanni's head snapped in the direction of the sound, a look of annoyance flashing across his face. Muttering something under his breath, he quickly left the alcove, his mind evidently now on other matters.

Antonio didn't dare move for what felt like an eternity, allowing his heart to return to normal and ensuring Giovanni was truly gone. Retrieving the pendant, he left a note for Liliana, suggesting they postpone their meeting. That night, he realised just how razor-thin the line between safety and exposure was. Their love wasn't just a risk; it was a high-stakes gamble against fate itself.

****

After that heart-stopping close call with Giovanni, Antonio and Liliana decided to take their meetings indoors, away from prying eyes. But even there, discretion was paramount. Liliana's chambers, adorned with lavish fabrics and intricate tapestries, had a window that overlooked a small, discreet courtyard. It was through this window, with the help of rope, that Antonio would often sneak into the embrace of his love.

As the moonlight painted the room with its silvery hue, they reunited. Their silhouettes danced upon the walls, two souls converging in a forbidden dance. The world outside ceased to exist; the politics of the city, the looming danger, all faded away. Their universe contracted to just the room, the silent rustle of silk sheets, and the warmth of each other's embrace.

The air was thick with tension and desire, intertwined like the intricate patterns on the drapes. Each touch, each gaze was a stanza in the poem of their love; every breath, a verse in the symphony of their passion. They moved together in a rhythm as old as time, yet as fresh and vibrant as the first bloom of spring. The sheets, soft and pliant, whispered secrets of their union, cradling them in its luxurious embrace.

As dawn's first light began to spill into the room, casting everything in a golden glow, they lay nestled together. Antonio's head rested on Liliana's chest, the gentle rise and fall of her breath a soothing lullaby. In the tranquility of the morning, they exchanged soft whispers, dreams of a future, and promises of eternal love.

But reality, as always, intruded upon their bliss. The first calls of the city's morning bustle reminded them of the perilous nature of their liason. With a heavy heart and a final lingering kiss, Antonio climbed out of the window, disappearing into the break of dawn, leaving Liliana with memories of another stolen night. The weight of their love and the ever-present dangers they faced added a bittersweet edge to their secret rendezvous, but for those few precious hours, they were simply two souls bound by love.

Chapter 13

The hidden palazzo had seen days of grandeur, and now, in its silent chambers, it bore witness to the passion and turmoil of Antonio's heart. Although the walls echoed with the sounds of preparations and whispered conspiracies, Antonio's chamber was a quiet haven. Here, he could be vulnerable, letting his guard down and allowing his heart to yearn openly.

By the window, where dappled sunlight filtered through, Antonio rested in contemplative silence. The golden light played on his features, revealing a face lost in deep thought. Each ray seemed to bring with it a memory of Liliana - her soft laughter, the gentle curve of her lips, the spark in her eyes that danced only for him. He closed his eyes, reliving their last stolen moment, the sensation of silk sheets, and the weight of her body entwined with his. He could still feel the gentle rise and fall of her chest as he lay with his head against her, their whispered words painting dreams in the dark.

These memories, though recent, felt like a lifeline in the sea of chaos that threatened to engulf him. With each meeting, the stakes grew higher, the danger more real. But the pull they felt towards each other, that inexplicable magnetic force, seemed to eclipse all reason and caution.

A sigh escaped his lips. His heart ached for their next rendezvous, for the promise of her touch and the solace he found in her embrace. Yet, juxtaposed with this longing was the weight of his mission, the need to reclaim what was taken from him and restore balance to Venice.

A soft knock on his chamber door brought him back from his reverie. Duty beckoned, and he was once again the leader, the mastermind, ready to face the challenges that lay ahead. But in the sanctuary of his heart, he carried with him the memory of Liliana, a bittersweet reminder of what was at stake.

****

The sound of footsteps and low voices gradually filled the palazzo's meeting room. A massive table dominated the centre, upon which maps, tools, and other objects of intrigue were spread out.

Lorenzo, the once trusted guard of Leonora but now an ally to Antonio, was the first to enter. With him came the unmistakable air of determination, evidence of the pivotal role he'd play in tonight's proceedings. Following closely were other loyal allies - cunning spies, experienced thieves, and strategists - each bringing a unique set of skills essential for the operation. Some were bound to Antonio by past favours, others by shared disdain for Leonora's rule, and a fe by the hope of a better Venice.

Antonio took his place at the head of the table, his eyes scanning each face. He saw the anticipation, the anxiety, and the resolve. They were about to embark on their most daring mission yet, one that was as much about restoring the soul of Venice as it was about the sapphire heirloom.

"With tonight's endeavour," Antonio began, his voice

filled with gravitas, "we're not only reclaiming what was unjustly taken but also sending a clear message to all of Venice. Leonora's reign, built on deceit and tyranny, will see its first crack. We will show them that the spirit of Venice remains unbroken."

Lorenzo unrolled a detailed blueprint of the Morosini residence. "The main entrance will be heavily guarded, but there are lesser-known passageways which we can exploit," he explained, pointing to a series of interconnected underground tunnels.

Another ally, a noble and stealthy thief known for her unparalleled ability to go undetected, chimed in, "The sapphire is rumoured to be kept in Leonora's private chamber, which has been fortified recently. But tonight, they host a grand ball. With the entire household and much of Venice distracted by the festivities, it's our best chance."

Antonio's expression tightened as he processed what she said. "Ball? Tonight?"

Lorenzo glanced hesitantly at Antonio, seeming to wrestle with his words. "Yes, the grand ball in celebration of Liliana's impending marriage to Duke of Alarico of Verona. It's tomorrow."

A silent tension settled over the room. Antonio's face went white as he fought to maintain composure. The revelation that Liliana was to marry another was like a dagger to his heart. The room seemed to grow colder, and the shadows cast by the candles danced menacingly. The atmosphere was thick with unspoken words and shared concerns. The very woman he was secretly seeing was about to be wedded to another, and that too, someone as powerful as the Duke of Verona.

Antonio took a deep breath, trying to keep his emotions in check. "Tonight's operation is more crucial than ever," he finally said, his voice laced with a steely determination that concealed his inner turmoil.

Lorenzo, recognising the need to move the conversation forward, added, "The ball will have most of the household and the guards occupied. It's the perfect diversion. We can get in, retrieve the sapphire, and get out before anyone is the wiser."

Someone from the crowed spoke up, "We'll need to blend in. Some of us should be among the guests. The rest can use the tunnels. Antonio, given the circumstances, it might be best if you stayed behind."

Antonio's gaze hardened. "I am not going to stand by while Liliana marries another. I will be there, in the heart of it all."

The group shared uneasy glances, recognising the immense personal stakes Antonio now had. The plan began to take shape, with some allies securing invitations to the ball while others readied themselves for the covert operation.

****

Antonio stood by the canalised, watching as his team meticulously packed a small Venetian boat with an array of tools and equipment. Masks designed to blend into the masquerade, each one ornate and detailed, yet crafted to ensure a quick escape if necessary. Sheathed daggers, cloaks, and ropes sat nestled amongst vials containing concoctions capable of rendering guards unconscious. Each item was chosen with precision, bearing testimony to the significance of their upcoming mission.

The waters of the canal reflected the first stars of the evening, gentle ripples spreading out as the boat was pushed away from the dock. Antonio took a seat at the helm, taking a moment to look up at the vast night sky, seeking some form of solace. But instead of peace, his thoughts were invaded by the image of Duke Alarico, the man who was to claim Liliana's hand in marriage. The thought made Antonio's grip on the oars tighten until his knuckles went white. The weight of Liliana's upcoming marriage to a man she did not love, especially one as influential and powerful as the Duke, consumed him.

Rowing in tandem with Lorenzo, the pair made their way silently through the canals. As they approached the Morosini estate, the distant sounds of laughter, music and the clinking of glasses painted a vivid picture of the festivities within. The grandeur of the Morosini estate loomed ahead, lights sparkling, its silhouette a haunting reminder of what Antonio had lost and what he stood to lose.

They docked the boat in a shadowed alcove, just out of view from the main thoroughfare but close enough for a swift infiltration. As Antonio tied the boat to a post, the weight of the evening pressed down on him, not just the heist but the personal vendetta that bubbled beneath the surface. The Duke, much like Leonora, though merely a player in a larger game, had become a symbol of all of

Antonio's losses, and tonight, the scales would be balanced one way or another, that much he was sure about.

Antonio and his team worked silently, their movements fluid and rehearsed. The boat's contents were unloaded with precision: each mask, weapon, and piece of equipment had its own and purpose. As they geared up, the glint of concealed blades and the rustle of cloaks were the only indicators of the deadly intent beneath their masked facades. Antonio, always one for flair, chose a mask adorned with feathers that danced with every movement, its intricate beadwork reflecting the moonlight. Lorenzo's mask was more subdued, its dark colours making him almost invisible in the shadows, save for the glint in his eyes.

Each member of the team checked their equipment, ensuring that ropes were coiled correctly, blades were sharp, and vials were secured. Mutual nodes exchanged between them indicated readiness. Antonio, lost in thought for a moment, glanced at the grand entrance of the estate, knowing Liliana was within those walls. The weight of their relationship, paired against the evening's agenda, was a burden he carried with every step.

Selecting a hidden corner with a clear view of the estate's entrance, the team positioned themselves strategically. The festivities were in full swing, with guests arriving in their finest attire, masks concealing identities, and laughter echoing into the night. The cacophony of the ball provided the perfect cover for Antonio and his crew. They watched as nobles, politicians, and influential figures of Venice made their entrance, the grandeur on display a stark reminder of the world Antonio once belonged to and the one he was fighting to reclaim.

From their vantage point, they observe the guards' patterns, noting the frequency of their rounds and any potential vulnerabilities. With every passing carriage and new arrival, the tension in the air thickened. Antonio's hand instinctively went to the hilt of his dagger whenever he thought he saw the figure of the Duke. But it was all a waiting game now, for that perfect moment when their infiltration could begin, under the cover of revelry and the guise of just another group of masqueraded guests.

****

The Morosini residence was alive with music, laughter, and the sound of merriment. Gilded chandeliers hung from the ceiling, their candles illuminating the grand hall with a soft, warm glow. The room was filled with a sea of swirling dresses and tailored suits, every guest trying to outdo the other in splendour and opulence. Musicians played a lively tune, the notes of their violins and flute intertwining seamlessly with the rhythm of tambourines and lutes.

At the heart of the ballroom, a large dance floor had been set up, and couples spun gracefully in tandem to the music, their steps impeccably synchronised. Above them, on a raised platform, say the hosts for the evening. Lady Leonora, looking regal in her gown of deep green velvet, was surrounded by a court of admirers hanging on her every word. But beside her, seated in a place of honour, was the guest of the evening, Duke Alarico. His sharp features were highlighted by a mask of deep purple and gold, and he wore a self-satisfied smirk, enjoying the festivities and the imminent promise of a beneficial union.

Liliana, radiant in a silver and lavender ensemble that complemented her dark locks, stood a little away, engaging in polite conversation with a closer of noblewomen. Her beauty was unparalleled, and many an eye in the room was drawn to her. Every so often, her gaze would flit towards the entrance, a subtle restlessness betraying her composure. She wasn't entirely sure why, but something felt out of place. She could feel it in her bones.

The scent of roasted meats and spiced wines wafted through the room from the banquet tables. Guests chatted animatedly, cups in hands, as they discussed the latest political intrigues, shared gossip, and speculated about the night's surprises.

Jesters danced playfully between the guests, their colourful costumes shimmering with every twirl, their antics drawing bouts of laughter from the crowd. Fire breathers showcased their skills in the courtyard, sending arcs of flame soaring into the night, their daring feats met with gasps and applause. Minstrels roamed, serenading groups with ballads of old, while poets recited tales of romance and chivalry, captivating listeners with their lyrical prowess.

The sumptuous spread laid out was a fast for the senses. Platters of roasted game, honey-glazed ham, and a myriad of fish dishes lay alongside bowls of fresh fruits and loaves of freshly baked bread. Delicate pastries and rich desserts tempted even the most restrained, while an assortment of cheeses paired perfectly with the variety of wines brought forth from the Morosini cellars.

As the night deepened, the mood grew more exhilarating. Guests took turns playing games of chance, wagering on the room of dice or the turn of a card. Others formed circles for spirited debates on art, literature, and philosophy.

Duke Alarico, sipping from a golden chalice, regaled a captive audience with tales of his homeland, his voice filled with pride and nostalgia. All the while, his eyes kept returning to Liliana, who gracefully flitted from one group to another, playing the role of the perfect hostess.

In a quieter corner, a gifted lute player began a melancholic tune, drawing couples to the dance floor. The gentle sway of bodies and the whispered endearments exchanged were a testament to the magic of the evening.

With an air of authority and purpose, Duke Alarico approached Liliana, extending his hand in an unspoken invitation. Her heart sank, but with a practiced smile she placed her hand in his. As they began to move, the room seemed to pause, all eyes on the couple, watching the merger of two powerful families play out in a dance.

"My dear Liliana," Alarico began, his voice dripping with feigned sweetness, "Tomorrow marks the day our fates intertwine, bringing prosperity to both our houses." He spun her around, his grip on her waist tighter than necessary.

She swallowed her unease and replied, choosing her words with care. "Indeed, Duke. It is a union of political and economic significance. Our families stand to benefit greatly."

His laughter, oily and dark, filled the air between them. "Ah, ever the diplomat. But let us not forget the more… personal advantages of our arrangement." His gaze slid over her, possessive and lecherous, making her skin crawl.

Desperate for a reprieve, Liliana tried to steer the conversation elsewhere. "The ball is a success. Your stories have enchanted the guests. Venice is eager to learn more about Verona."

His grip tightened further, pulling her close, so their faces were mere inches apart. "Venice should be eager for our union, as should you," he whispered, his breath reeking of wine.

Internally, Liliana recoiled, memories of Antonio flooding her mind, amplifying her revulsion toward the Duke. How she yearned for Antonio's gentle touch, his genuine warmth. But she masked her disgust with practiced ease. "Of course, Duke. It is all for the greater good."

The Duke smirked, seeming to drink in her beauty as they continued their dance. "Ah, Liliana, you may try to hide it, but I can sense your eagerness. Together, we shall be the envy of all of Venice."

Just as Liliana was about to reply, a voice rang out, smooth and confident, cutting through the music. "Excuse me, Duke. Might I have this dance?"

The Duke's brow furrowed in annoyance, but upon seeing the speaker, a tall- dark-haired figured with an air of confidence, his expression turned to one of curiosity. "And who might you be?"

The mysterious man gave a slight bow, "A humble guest, eager to share a dance with the beautiful bride-to-be."

Intrigued by the audacity and drunk enough to be easily persuaded, the Duke released Liliana, a smirk playing on his lips. "Very well, but remember, she is mine come tomorrow."

With a final predatory gaze, the Duke wandered off, looking for another unsuspecting guest to ensnare.

The mysterious man took Liliana's hand, pulling her close. The music swelled around them, but Liliana was more attuned to the warmth emanating from her dance partner, the strong yet gentle grip on her hand, and the comfort she felt, which was all too familiar.

For a moment, the world faded. The ballroom, the guests, the looming wedding - everything vanished. It was just her and this man, their bodies moving in perfect harmony.

"Who are you?" she whispered, unable to shake the feeling of deja vu.

He leaned in, his lips brushing against her ear, his voice barely audible above the music. "Someone who would move heaven and earth for you."

Liliana's heart raced. Was it possible? Could it be? She tried to get a clearer look at the man's face, but his mask concealed his identity, leaving her with more questions than answers.

The rhythm of the dance, coupled with the mysterious man's presence, had an intoxicating effect on Liliana. Every step, every spin, every whispered word felt like a dream she didn't want to wake from. The man led her gracefully across the floor, drawing both awe and envy from onlookers.

But as the song began its final chords, a sense of urgency seemed to emanate from him. Their movement began to edge closer to a dimly lit exit, away from the prying eyes of the main ballroom.

Liliana, caught up in the embrace and the enigma of her partner, hardly noticed. "I feel like I know you," she murmured, her eyes searching his for any hint of recognition.

The masked man paused, pulling her closer. His gaze, even behind the mask, held a depth of emotion she found both comforting and heartbreaking. "In another life, perhaps," he whispered, his voice quivering ever so slightly.

Just then, a clock began to chime, signalling midnight. It was as if the sound broke the spell they were under. The man suddenly stiffened, pulling away abruptly. "I'm sorry," he said, regret evident in his voice. "I must go."

Before Liliana could protest or ask any questions, he was gone, blending into the shadows and leaving her standing, dazed and heart pounding, in the middle of the dance floor.

On the periphery of the grand hall, Antonio swiftly removed his mast, the familiar weight of duty settling on him once more. He slipped into a side corridor, making his way to the agreed rendezvous point with his team. They had a plan to execute, and time was of the essence.

****

In the dimly lit corridor, Antonio met with Lorenzo, who was already adjusting his disguise - a servant's attire, complete with a tray of champagne flutes, intended to blend in seamlessly with the mansion's staff.

"Everything in place?" Antonio inquired, his voice barely audible.

Lorenzo nodded, handing Antonio a similar servant's outfit. "The others are spread throughout the crowd. We'll be virtually invisible. But remember, the moment things go south, we need to signal to alert them."

Antonio pulled out a small, ornate whistle, delicately crafted. "This will do the trick. Three short blows, and they'll converge."

The pair quickly dressed, then Lorenzo briefed Antonio on the layout he'd managed to gather from overhearing the staff's conversations. They would have to navigate a series of hallways, avoid guards, and finally, get to the chamber where the heirloom was rumoured to be displayed.

As Antonio and Lorenzo moved deeper into the mansion, they utilised every trick they knew - blending in with the flow of servants, mirroring their actions, using shadows to their advantage, and occasionally causing minor distractions to divert attention.

They came across the grand library, an ornate door slightly ajar. Beyond it was the sound of hushed voices. The duo peeked inside, spotting Duke Alarico in a compromising position with a lady not his bride-to-be. The Duke's lecherous actions confirmed what Liliana and Antonio already knew of his character.

This provided a golden opportunity. Lorenzo discreetly knocked over a vase in the corridor, drawing attention to the guards. "Apologies, my lord!" he exclaimed, diverting the attention of the Duke and the lady. This allowed Antonio to slip past the door and into the adjoining chamber where the heirloom was said to be.

There it was - a grand display in the centre of the room. The sapphire glinted under the candlelight, causing an azure glow around. The weight of the moment pressed on Antonio. Here, in this chamber, lay the object of so many desires, the pivot on which fortunes would turn.

Lorenzo, realising Antonio's absence, played his part perfectly, apologising profusely and then retreating, leaving the Duke slightly irritated but none the wiser.

Inside the chamber, Antonio carefully approached the display, tools at the ready. But as he reached out, a reflection caught his eye - an insignia, eerily familiar. It belonged to Giovanni. The game had changed. Antonio's heart raced as he realised the heirloom was likely guarded by more than just locks - it was booby-trapped.

His mind raced, weighing his options. Outside, Lorenzo's sense of unease grew, his instincts telling him something wasn't right. Just then, a muffled sound echoed through the mansion - Antonio's whistle. Three short blows.

The room was filled with the distant hum of the ball, but in the immediate surroundings, there was only silence - a suffocating, tension-filled silence. Antonio's fingers trembled as he eyed the heirloom, the intricate mechanism surrounding it an indicator of its lethal defence. Taking a deep breath, he reached out, attempting to disarm the trap.

However, inexperience betrayed him. As he made contact, a sharp blade shot out, embedding itself into his arm. Antonio stifled a scream, clenching his teeth. Using his other hand, he managed to grab the sapphire heirloom, blood staining its magnificent blue.

As Antonio staggered out of the chamber, his vision blurred from both pain and exertion, the opulent hallway seemed to swim around him. Gilded frames bearing portraits of Morosini ancestors glinted in the dim candlelight, each face staring down in silent judgment. The weight of the heirloom in his hand was a cold reminder of the price he'd just paid, and the debt that was still due.

His heart, already racing from his brush with the trap, jumped as he nearly collided with a figure ahead. The Duke was sprawled inelegantly in a grand, high-backed chair, the rich fabrics of his clothing contrasting sharply with his undignified position. His face was flushed from wine, a thin trail of drool escaping the corner of his mouth. The goblet he'd been drinking from dangled precariously from lax fingers, threatening to tip and spill its ruby contents onto the white marble floor.

A cocktail of emotions churned in Antonio. Here was the man slated to marry his beloved Liliana. He remembered her face earlier that evening, the mask of politeness barely concealing her disgust. The knowledge of their impending union gnawed at Antonio's insides, a festering wound that no balm could soothe.

This breaths became shallow, heart pounding loudly in his ears, each beat echoing the hurt and betrayal he felt. And now, in this silent corridor, with no witnesses, the opportunity to end it all presented itself.

With a fluidity that belied his injury, Antonio drew his dagger, its polished blade catching the candlelight, reflecting his tumultuous emotions. Time seemed to stretch, every detail sharp and vivid, from the soft snores of the Duke to the distant sounds of laughter and music from the ballroom.

He thought of Liliana, of their stolen moments, and the future they could never have if the Duke remains in the picture. With a swift, decisive motion, the weight on Antonio's heart was momentarily lifted, replaced by the cold finality of what he'd just done. The Duke would never wake from his drunken stupor.

The weight of his act pressed heavily upon Antonio's heart as he hastily sheathed his dagger and tried to regain some semblance of composure. The hallways, which had been a maze during his entry, now seemed even more confusing as panic muddled his senses. Antonio knew he had to move quickly and escape before the crime was discovered.

Rounding a corner, he halted, shock rendering him momentarily paralysed. Lorenzo stood there, looking both apologetic and resigned. Beside him were Giovanni, eyes ablaze with fury, Liliana, her face a portrait of grief, and the imposing figure of Leonora, her lips curled in a triumphant sneer.

Lorenzo, whose friendship and alliance Antonio had never once doubted, had turned against him. The betrayal cut deeper than the physical pain from the trap.

"You thought it would be that easy, Antonio?" Leonora's voice dripped with scorn. "Did you really believe you could waltz into my home, steal what belongs to me, and walk away?"

Liliana's eyes searched Antonio's, a torrent of emotions playing in them: shock, pain, love, and a deep sense of betrayal. "Antonio," she whispered, the pain evident in her voice, "why?"

Antonio took a deep breath, summoning his remaining strength. "It was never about the heirloom, it was about freedom. Your freedom from this wretched arrangement. Your mother has you ensnared in her web of politics and deceit."

"Such noble intentions," Leonora mocked. "And yet, in your quest for her freedom, you've signed her over to a lifetime of captivity."

Antonio's gaze shifted to Lorenzo. "Why?" he asked, the single word laced with a depth of betrayal.

Lorenzo looked down, unable to meet Antonio's eyes. "She promised me a future, Antonio. A position of power. I… I didn't think it would come to this."

Just then, a scream echoed from the corridor - the lifeless body of the Duke had been found.

Leonora's eyes darkened, her lips pulling back in rage. "Look at what you've done," she hissed.

Giovanni seethed, stepping forward. "You've gone too far."

Leonora, her eyes never leaving Antonio's, said, "Kill him."

Giovanni and Lorenzo hesitated, both grappling with their emotions and the gravity of the command. Liliana stepped forward, her voice desperate. "Mother, no!"

Leonora's eyes fixated on the sapphire in Antonio's hand, a glint of malevolence flashing in her gaze. An otherworldly energy emanated from her, her posture becoming rigid, her expression transforming into one of pure malice. As though drawn by the sapphire itself, a dark, almost demonic force seemed to possess her. The opulent surroundings faded, and all that remained was the relentless pull of the stone compelling her forward.

Around them, the air grew heavy, suffocating, as if the very walls of the Morosini residence bore witness to the impending tragedy. A chilling whisper, emanating from the sapphire or perhaps from some ancient curse, seemed to beckon Leonora, urging her, "End him."

Time seemed to distort, each second stretching into an eternity. Antonio could only watch in paralysed horror as Leonora, driven by an evil force, closed the distance between them with supernatural speed. The world became a blur, but the glint of her dagger was unmistakable, catching the soft glow of the chandeliers as it raced towards his throat, her other hand snatching the bloodied sapphire away.

As the cold steel bit into his flesh, the world grew hazy and sounds grew distant. But one sound was impossible to miss - Liliana's heart-wrenching, unearthly scream of despair. It echoed through the halls, resonating with a pain so profound that it seemed as if her very soul was shattering. She crumpled to the ground, her delicate fingers clutching at her chest, tears streaming down her face, a picture of unspeakable grief.

Giovanni, in his shock, tried to reach for his sister, but the weight of the moment, the sheer intensity of emotions, left everyone frozen, ensnared in the tragedy that had just played out before their eyes.

Silence blanketed the room, punctuated only by the low, mournful sobs of Liliana. The lavish decorations and shimmering lights of the ballroom seemed grotesquely inappropriate now, mocking the raw anguish that gripped the room. The scent of spiced wines and roasted meats turned sickly in the throes of death.

Giovanni, wrestling with his own shock, attempted to pull Liliana into an embrace, trying to shield her from the grim reality of Antonio's lifeless body. But she resisted, her eyes locked on Antonio, her face a mask of disbelief.

Lorenzo, realising the true nature of the chaos and the betrayal that had taken place, slowly began to back away, his eyes darting toward the nearest exit. He had always been loyal to Leonora, but seeing the aftermath of her unbridled fury, he couldn't help but question his allegiances.

Leonora, meanwhile, stood over Antonio's body, a mixture of satisfaction and madness dancing in her eyes. The sapphire's pull was evident, its corrupting influence having taken root. It was as if she had tapped into some dark, ancient power, one that both emboldened and consumed her.

Across the room, a few guests who had been far enough from the scene to avoid the immediate shock began to murmur, whispers of horror and confusion spreading like wildfire. Some were frozen in place, their faces aghast, while others made hasty exists, wanting no part in the unfolding drama.

Liliana, eyes red and swollen from crying, rose unsteadily to her feet. Her gaze turned to Leonora, her mother, now her enemy.

"You," Liliana whispered, voice trembling with rage. "You have taken everything from me."

Leonora, though still entranced by the power of the sapphire, hesitated for a split second upon hearing her daughter's voice. The human part of her, buried deep beneath the influence of the gem, yearned to reach out and comfort her. But the dark power flowing through her veins was too strong, drowning out any remnants of maternal instinct.

Giovanni stepped between the two women, his eyes darting from one to the other, trying to diffuse the situation. "Liliana, step back. Mother, give me the stone. It's corrupted you!"

Leonora's laugh was a cruel, echoing sound in the room, contrasting the horrified silence of the remaining guests. "You think this is corruption? No, this is power, the likes of which our family has never known. And I will not relinquish it."

Suddenly, a loud crash resonated through the hall. One of Antonio's allies, having witnessed the murder, had thrown a smoke bomb into the centre of the room. Thick, obscuring smoke billowed out, creating a temporary shield.

Taking advantage of the chaos, Lorenzo, his loyalty to Leonora forever shattered, beckoned to the remaining members of Antonio's team. Together, they fled the ballroom, vanishing into the night.

Leonora's escape was swift. As the smoke billowed throughout the room, obscuring vision and filling the senses with its acrid scent, most guests were consumed by confusion and panic. But Leonora, driven by the dark power of the sapphire, moved with purpose. Darting through a side door, her dress rustling in her wake, she made her way through the corridors of her ancestral estate.

Her heart raced, but it was no longer out of fear. It was exhilaration. The gem around her neck pulsed with energy, amplifying her emotions and urging her forward.

Reaching her private chamber, she slammed the door shut, locking it behind her. The room, bathed in the dim glow of candlelight, felt both familiar and foreign. The portraits of her ancestors looked down on her with judgment, their eyes following her every move. Leonora scarcely noticed them. The walked to the large bay window that overlooked the estate's sprawling gardens.

Outside, chaos reigned. Guests, once clad in elegant gowns and sharp tuxedos, now fled in disarray, their finery stained and torn. Their screams of terror were carried away by the wind, joining the cacophony of the gathering storm. Dark clouds rolled in, each rumble of thunder resonating with the turmoil in Leonora's heart.

As she stared out, the rain began to fall - fierce and relentless. It streaked the windowpanes, blurring outside into a water tableau of panic and despair.

Leonora reached up, touching the sapphire that hung heavily around her neck. The gem was warm, its facets slick with a substance that gleamed in the candlelight. Blood. Antonio's blood. As it dripped, each droplet seemed to sizzle and evaporate before hitting the floor.

Her reflection in the windowpane was a distorted version of the woman she once was. The power of the sapphire had consumed her, its essence intertwining with her very soul. Her eyes, once vibrant, now glowed with an unnatural luminescence. The corners of her lips twitched into a cruel smile. She felt invincible.

As the tempest raged outside, Leonora's transformation was complete. No longer the respected matriarch of the Morosini family, she had become something far more dangerous. The storm inside her mirrored the storm outside, and Venice would never be the same again.

Chapter 14

The sun had barely risen over Venice, casting a soft golden hue over its structures. The city's usual serene beauty was no overshadowed by an atmosphere thick with dread. The waters, typically glistening, bore witness to hurried conversations and tense exchanges.

Whispers spread like wildfire, carried by the wind from one end of the city to the other. Every alleyway, every market square, every bridge, was abuzz with hushed tones. "Did you hear about the Morosini residence?" one fishmonger asked another as they set up their stalls in the Rialto market.

"The Duke of Verona, dead? And by an assassin's blade in the heart of Venice!" explained a noblewoman to her maid, her voice trembling with a mixture of thrill and horror. The maid shushed her, eyes darting around to ensure no one else had overheard.

At the Doge's palace, council members convened for an emergency session, their faces grave. The stability of the city was at stake. With the Duke's unexpected death and the tales of dark magic surrounding the Morosini family heirloom, alliances would be tested, and Venice's political landscape could shift dramatically.

Children, sensing the unease of their elders but not fully understanding the gravity of the situation, asked innocent questions that were met with hushed responses and averted eyes. Their games in the streets were more subdued, their laughter a little less carefree.

As the day wore on, boats filled the Grand Canal, but not with tourists or merchants. Instead, they carried worried citizens seeking answers or perhaps an escape from the impending storm.

The taverns, which had always been the heartbeat of the city, became places of contemplation. Candle flames flickered in the dimly lit interiors, casting shadows on the worn wooden tables and stone walls. The usual sounds of clinking glasses, hearty laugher, and boisterous songs were replaced by a stifling silence that seemed to smother the establishments. Every so often, the silence would be punctuated by a soft sigh, the scrape of a chair, or the gentle splash of wine being poured.

Bards and minstrels, who usually regaled the crowds with tales of heroism, love, and adventure, sat idly, their instruments untouched. The weight of recent events left them hesitant, unsure of which song or tale would be appropriate to soothe the heavy hearts of the patrons. Their eyes often wandered to the entrance, half expecting someone to burst in with news, updates or perhaps just a simple distraction from the bleak atmosphere.

In the corners of these taverns, older denizens who had witnessed Venice's many ups and downs over the decades exchanged knowing glances. They sipped their drinks slowly, deep in thought, perhaps reminiscing about past challenges the city had faced or pondering the inevitable changes this recent tragedy might bring.

The canals outside mirrored the mood inside the taverns. The usually shimmering waters looked darker, reflecting the heavy clouds that hung overhead. Gondolas moved languidly, their gondoliers propelling them forward with a certain melancholy, as if the rhythm of the city itself had slowed down, gripped by the unknown.

From the shadows of one such gloomy tavern, two figures emerged. Giovanni, his face etched with grief and determination, walked with a pace that was somewhere between a march and a mournful trudge. Beside him, Liliana moved with a grace that belied her sorrow. The tragic events at the Morosini residence weighed heavily on them both, the pain evident in their eyes and posture. Every corner of the city, every reflection in the waters, seemed to echo Antonio's haunting presence.

Liliana's shawl, draped over her shoulder, flapped softly in the evening breeze as she paused by the edge of a canal, gazing at the undulating water. The ripples, catching the dying light, painted fleeting pictures of that ill-fated night. Giovanni joined her, placing a protective arm around her shoulders. They both understood the gravity of their situation. Their city was in turmoil and the core of that chaos resided in their very home.

A somber realisation was dawning upon them. Their mother, Lenora, once a beacon of strength and guidance, was now ensnared by the curse of the sapphire heirloom. Every tale they had heard of its malevolent influence seemed to be manifesting before their very eyes. With each passing moment, Leonora was slipping further away, consumed by a power that was ancient, dark, and uncontrollable.

The siblings exchanged a wordless glance, a shared understanding passing between them. Memories of a happier time, when their family was united and untouched by malevolent forces, flooded their minds. But those days felt like another lifetime, lost to the sands of time. Now, a harsh truth was crystallising: the key to the city's salvation, and perhaps their own, lay in confronting Leonora. They would have to face the matriarch of the Morosini family, their own flesh and blood, and somehow free her from the heirloom's grip. The path ahead was fraught with danger, but the decision was clear. It was a confrontation they could no longer avoid.

The Morosini residence loomed before them, its grandeur and opulence now appearing eerie under the shroud of the recent events. Gone were the laughter and merry tunes of the ball; in their place was an ominous silence, punctuated only by the soft lapping of waters against the mansion's foundation. Every window was dark, the interior seemingly devoid of life, but the siblings knew that was far from the truth.

As they approached the main entrance, Giovanni cautiously felt for the concealed blade he had tucked into his belt earlier. Liliana clutched a small vial of liquid - a concoction known to weaken the strength of those it touched, in hopes it might aid them in subduing their mother without causing her harm.

The grand doors of the residence stood slightly ajar, the interior engulfed in shadow. Taking a deep breath, the two stepped inside. They were immediately met with signs of struggle and disarray: overturned furniture, shattered vases, and torn drapes painted a picture of Leonora's uncontrolled rage and the power the heirloom now held over her.

Moving silently, the duo navigated through the familiar yet now foreboding halls of their childhood home. Every creak of the wooden floor, every rustle of the wind outside made their hearts race. They knew that, under the sapphire's influence, Leonora was no longer the mother they once knew. The stories spoke of the heirloom's ability to amplify the darkest desires, twisting and corrupting the soul it ensnared.

Reaching Leonora's chamber door, they paused, exchanging a hesitant look. From within, they could hear a faint, melodic hum - a lullaby their mother used to sing to them as children. But now, it sounded distorted, filled with a sorrow and malevolence that sent shivers down their spines.

Liliana pressed her ear to the door, trying to gauge their mother's state. She whispered to Giovanni, "We need a plan." And he nodded in agreement. Before they could discuss further, a sudden crash from inside the chamber startled them.

Liliana and Giovanni exchanged a quick, determined glance before pushing the heavy chamber doors open. The room was dim, the only light emanating from the ominous glow of the sapphire heirloom, still stained with blood, which hung prominently around Leonora's neck. It pulsed faintly, casting eerie blue shadows across the room.

The source of the commotion was immediately apparent: an ornate mirror, once a proud fixture of Leonora's chambers, now lay shattered on the ground, its fragmented reflections showing glimpses of a disheveled, wild-eyes Leonora. She stood at the room's centre, hands clenched, breathing heavily. Her gaze, when it fell upon her children, wasn't one of recognition but of vague curiosity, as though she was looking at strangers.

"It seems I have guests," she murmured, her voice dripping with an uncanny coldness. "How unexpected."

Giovanni stepped forward, voice firm, though not without a tremble, "Mother, it's us. Liliana and Giovanni. Please, we're here to help."

Leonora's lips curled into a cruel smirk, the sapphire's glow intensifying momentarily. "Help?" she echoed, voice dripping with disdain. "No one can help me now."

Liliana, tears forming in her eyes, spoke softly, "We have heard of the sapphire's power, its curse. Let us help you break free from it. We don't want to lose you."

Leonora's laughter, magic and echoing, filled the chamber. "Lose me? Oh, my dear, you never had me. Not once this stone chose me."

The siblings could see the battle within their mother - moments of clarity where the real Leonora seemed to shine through, only to be swallowed by the dark power of the heirloom. The realisation dawned upon them that a direct confrontation would be catastrophic. They needed a more strategic approach, possible finding a way to separate Leonora from the heirloom or weaken its control.

Backing away slowly, Giovanni signalled to Liliana, hinting towards a tactical retreat. "We will return, Mother," he promised, his voice unwavering. "And when we do, we'll free you from this nightmare."

Leonora, or the entity that controlled her, simply watched them, an enigmatic smile playing on her lips, as the siblings retreated from the chamber, already formulating a plan to save their family from the ensnaring grip the curse had on them.

****

The vaulted ceilings of the old Venetian library towered overhead, shelves stretching high into the shadows, filled with manuscripts, scrolls, and tomes of forgotten lore. Dust particles danced in the few beams of sunlight that managed to filter through the tall, stained-glass windows, casting the space in a solemn, amber glow.

Liliana and Giovanni sat at a heavy wooden table, scattered with books and scrolls whose pages were yellowed by time. Each volume detailed legends, prophecies, and accounts of the sapphire's storied history. With every passing minute, their horror grew as they unraveled the terrible truth.

One ancient manuscript, bound in worn leather, described the sapphire's origins, detailing how it was forged in the heart of a fallen star and had since been the bane of countless empires. It was said that whoever possessed the stone would be granted unimaginable power, but at the cost of their very soul, becoming a puppet to the sapphire's age-old malevolence.

Another scroll spoke of a king who, under the stone's influence, turned against his own people, drowning his city in blood and fire before the stone moved on to its next victim, leaving devastation in its wake.

"I always believed these were mere tales," Giovanni muttered, his fingers tracing the intricate illustrations depicting the stone's past wielders, each figure surrounded by scenes of chaos and despair. "Stories meant to frighten children."

Liliana, her face pale from the weight of their discoveries, whispered, "But it's all true. Every word. This is no ordinary gem, and our battle isn't merely with Mother. We're facing an ancient evil, one that has plagued humanity for eons. I never knew such things existed, I always thought they were myths, fairytales."

Giovanni's determination hardened. "Then we'll need a plan."

Liliana glanced at the vast array of manuscripts and scrolls, her eyes tired but full of purpose. "More than that. We need allies. We can't hope to face the power of the sapphire and Mother alone."

She was right. No matter their personal resolve, they were up against a force that had swayed kings and razed entire cities. "Do you think there's anyone left who would stand with us?"

Liliana hesitated, her mind racing. "Lorenzo."

Giovanni raised an eyebrow. "You can't possible mean to trust him? After everything that's happened?"

She nodded. "We have no choice. He may have been misled by Leonora, but deep down, he knows the truth. Besides, he's seen the effects of the sapphire firsthand."

With a shared determination, the siblings ventured into the alleys and shadowed corners of the city, following whispers and hints until they found themselves at a nondescript palazzo. Its sign bore a familiar insignia, one that belonged to Antonio and his allies: a silver bell.

Inside, the atmosphere was tense. Hushed conversations ceased as they entered, all eyes on them. And at the far end of the dimly lit room, they found Lorenzo. He was different - a changed man. The once proud and laughter demeanour had been replaced by a seriousness, a weight of responsibility. He was now the leader of Antonio's old band.

Upon seeing them, he stood, his expression inscrutable. "You've come," he said simply.

"We need your help," Liliana began, her voice wavering slightly.

Lorenzo glanced around the room, taking in the faces of the men and women who had once stood alongside Antonio. "I've seen what that cursed stone has done. And I've pledged my loyalty to this cause, not to Leonora."

Giovanni took a deep breath, "Then, together, we'll free our mother and our city from the heirloom's grasp."

Lorenzo stepped forward, the candlelight casting shadows on his face. "The stone's corruption runs deep, deeper than any of us could've imagined. Leonora is no longer the mother you once knew."

Liliana swallowed hard, fighting back the tears. "That's why we must act swiftly, for her sake and for Venice."

A burly man at the corner table, scarred by countless battles, stood up. "Antonio might be gone, but his vision lives on. We're with you."

The room murmured in agreement. It was clear that the loyalty Antonio had inspired in his allies was now extended to his cause, to the siblings, and to saving their city.

Lorenzo unfurled a map of Venice on the table, pointing out key locations. "While we confront Leonora and the sapphire's power, we must also ensure the safety of the citizens. The heirloom's influence is unpredictable. We don't know how far its power can reach."

As they began to discuss strategies, the tavern door slammed open, sending a chilling gust through the room. A disheveled messenger stumbled in, gasping for breath. "The Doge's Palace!" he explained. "Leonora… she's taken control of it."

Giovanni's eyes widened. "What has she done?"

The messenger, trying to catch his breath, stuttered, "She has… commanded that the Grand Canal be dammed, diverting its waters straight towards the heart of the city. Without the canal's flow, the city's very foundations are at risk. Buildings will crumble, the city will flood! Venice will be destroyed!"

The room fell silence, the weight of the situation heavy in the air. Taking the Grand Canal was not just a strategic move; it was a statement. With Venice's lifeblood under threat, the city's very survival was now hanging in the balance. It was clear that under the sapphire's influence, Leonora would stop at nothing to consolidate her power, even if it meant the destruction of the city she once loved.

Shockwaves of disbelief ran through the palazzo's occupants. The Grand Canal was the heartbeat of the city; its waterways were the lifeblood of commerce, communication, and transportation. To disrupt its flow was to choke the city itself.

Lorenzo's face paled, realising the gravity of Leonora's move. "This isn't just about power. The sapphire is aiming to reshape Venice, to hold it according to its whims."

Liliana's fingers tightened around the edge of the table. "We can't let that happen. Venice is our home. We have to save it, even if it means going against our own blood."

Giovanni nodded grimly. "First, we need to stop the damming. Lorenzo, can your allies manage that?"

Lorenzo thought for a moment, surveying the room. "Yes, but it will be dangerous. The damming site will undoubtedly be heavily guarded."

A voice from the back called out, "For Venice, we'll brave any danger." Others murmured their agreement, their resolve unyielding.

Giovanni, appreciative of the support, continued. "We'll also need to confront our mother at the Doge's Palace. We need to free her from the heirloom's grasp."

The plans were quickly laid out. While a group of Antonio's allies would covertly approach the damming site, attempting to reverse or at least stall the progress, the Morosini siblings, backed by a select few, would infiltrate the Doge's Palace.

Time was of the essence. Every passing moment meant Venice edged closer to destruction. As the groups dispersed to prepare, Liliana took a moment to reflect, clutching the pendant Antonio had once gifted her. She whispered a silent prayer, not just for their success, but for the salvation of their mother's soul.

With the moonlight as their guide, the group traversed the canals of the city. The closer they drew to the Doge's Palace, the denser the atmosphere became, weighed down with foreboding.

The palace itself, usually an emblem of grandeur and

authority, now seemed like a looming fortress, casting long shadows over the water. The intricate marble facades, which once gleamed with pride, now seemed cold and unwelcoming.

As they approached, Lorenzo signalled for them to dock at a lesser-known entry point, a secret water gate used in times past for clandestine meetings and covert operations. It was a testament to Antonio's intelligence network that they knew of it. As they disembarked, Liliana couldn't help but think of Antonio and the many covert operations he'd led. She shook her head, forcing herself to focus on the task at hand.

Navigating the palace's corridors stealthily, they relied on Lorenzo's knowledge. He had been here countless times as a confidante of their mother before their heirloom had ensnared her. His familiarity with the layout proved invaluable.

The hallways, usually bustling with courtiers and guests, were eerily silent, the only sound their footsteps echoing softly against the marble. As they journeyed deeper, the could feel a change in the air - a chilling energy that seemed to radiate from the very walls.

Suddenly, as they rounded a corner, they were met with a sight that took their breath away. A grand chamber lay before them, its high vaulted ceiling adorned with intricate frescoes, now bathed in an otherworldly blue glow emanating from the centre of the room.

There, on a raised dais, stood Leonora. Her figure, usually so full of regal poise, was now transformed. Draped in deep blue robes that seemed to ripple and shimmer, her eyes reflected the same eerie luminescence of the sapphire heirloom hanging prominently around her neck. It pulsed with a malevolent light, casting ghostly reflections onto the chamber's walls, daring anybody who wished for their demise to approach.

Leonora's voice, once warm and nurturing, echoed chillingly through the chamber. "Ah, my dear children, you've finally come." Her smile, however, was not one of maternal affection, but a sinister, mocking curve of the lips, the malevolent force within her evident.

Lorenzo took a step forward, determination evident in his eyes. "Leonora, you must free yourself from this cursed gem's grip! Remember your family, remember Venice!"

Leonora's laughter filled the chamber, a haunting sound that made the group shudder. "Poor, naive Lorenzo. You think this is merely the gem's doing? It has only amplified what was already within me."

Liliana, tears in her eyes, said, "Mother, we know you're in there. We'll do whatever it takes to free you from its influence."

Leonora looked at her daughter, her gaze cold and detached. "And what would you know of its power? Of the endless possibilities it presents? It has shown me a vision, Liliana, a Venice where the Morosini family reigns supreme."

Giovanni clenched his fists. "That's not our mother speaking. We need to act now."

Before he could make a move, Lorenzo lunged at Leonora, attempting to snatch the sapphire. But Leonora, with a speed that seemed inhuman, sidestepped him. With a flick of her wrist, Lorenzo was sent hurtling across the room, crashing into the stone wall with a sickening thud. He slumped to the ground, lifeless.

A collective gasp echoed throughout the chamber. Liliana's scream pierced the silence, raw and full of anguish. She ran to Lorenzo's side, cradling his head, tears flowing freely down her face. "No, no, no," she whispered, voice broken, "Not you too."

Leonora looked on with cold detachment, her laughter a chilling contrast to the scene of grief in front of her. "You should've known better," she sneered.

Giovanni, his face contorted in pain and rage, drew his weapon. "This ends now, Leonora!"

Antonio's allies rallied, their previous hesitation gone, replaced with a fiery determination. But as they advanced, Leonora's voice echoed through the vast hall, carrying a power that was otherworldly. "Enough!" And with that single command, the windows and doors slammed shut, and an impenetrable darkness descended, plunging the chamber into utter blackness.

Moments later, when light returned, Leonora was nowhere to be found. The group, disoriented and in shock, began to gather together. Amidst the sorrow and rage, one thing was clear: Leonora was not just their enemy, but a formidable force of darkness that threatened all of Venice.

Liliana, her grief giving way to determination, rose from Lorenzo's side. Wiping away her tears, she looked at Giovanni. "We need to find her and end this."

Giovanni nodded, his voice filled with resolve. "And we will. Together."

****

Utilising the vast network of contacts and allies Antonio had built over the years, the group managed to track down a renowned gem cutter named Fabrizio. An old man with wise eyes and trembling hands, Fabrizio had an uncanny skill in recreating the most precious of gems.

Liliana, holding a rough sketch of the sapphire heirloom, presented it to him. "We need an exact replica of this," she said. "It's our only chance."

Fabrizio examined the drawing closely, his brow furrowed. "I've heard tales of this tone," he muttered. "Crafting its likeness will be a challenge, but for the sake of Venice I will try."

While Fabrizio set to work, diligently crafting the replica, the group gathered around ancient blueprints of the palace, meticulously tracing out paths and strategising their next move. Candles burned low, casting flickering shadows on their focused faces.

Through trusted sources, they discovered Leonora's new patterns. It was said she often withdrew to a secluded, heavily fortified chamber at dusk, the room humming with a mysterious energy. This, they believed, was her tapping further into the sapphire's ominous powers. That vulnerable moment would be their best opportunity.

However, as the plans unfurled, a division grew amongst the group. Some believed that, should the switch fail, they needed to be prepared to kill Leonora to protect Venice. Others held onto the hope of saving her, adamant that they shouldn't resort to murder, especially when it involved family.

A particularly heated debated erupted one evening. Rafael, one of Antonio's oldest allies, argued fiercely. "We must consider the greater good! If the switch fails, we cannot let that cursed stone continue its reign through Leonora."

But Liliana, her voice quivering with emotion, countered, "She's our mother, Rafael. There has to be another way. The heirloom has taken her, but she's still in there somewhere."

Giovanni found himself torn. He understood the weight of the situation and the responsibility they bore to their city, but the thought of harming his own mother was unbearable. "We'll do everything we can to avoid that fate," he murmured, more to himself than to the group.

Night after night, as Fabrizio worked on the gem, the group grappled with the moral dilemma. The room was often filled with passionate arguments, moments of reflective silence, and shared tears.

****

The final touches on the replica were a marvel. Under Fabrizio's skilled hands, it was almost impossible to distinguish the faux sapphire from the genuine heirloom. Even its lustrous glow mimicked the otherworldly light of the original.

They gathered around a table, the false gem glistening in the candlelight, its light paired against the heavy weight of their mission. They needed an occasion, a moment when Leonora would be distracted enough for them to make the switch.

As if on cure, a whispered rumour began to circulate through the streets of Venice. Leonora had called for a grand assembly in a few days, at the heart of the city, and the grand Piazza San Marco. Whispers said she planned to usher in a "new age" for Venice, a change that many feared given her recent erratic and tyrannical behaviour.

This was the opportunity they had been waiting for.

They sprung into action, planning every minute detail. As the day of the assembly approached, the allies went undercover, blending seamlessly with the city's artisans, entertainers, and traders. It allowed them to position themselves advantageously around the Piazza.

Liliana would take on the guise of a performer, her natural grace and talent as a dancer making her blend seamlessly with a troupe scheduled to entertain. This would position her close to Leonora.

Giovanni would dress as a guard, moving through the crowd, ensuring their safety, and watching for any unexpected threats. Others in their group would mix within the crowd, ready to act as decoys, create diversions, or assist as needed.

The day arrived with a heavy, overcast sky, matching the tension that hung thick in the air. The grand Piazza was adorned with flags and banners, the city's emblem replaced with an emblem of the sapphire. Musicians played, but their tunes carried a nervous energy.

Leonora stepped onto the grand balcony overlooking the square. Adorned in regal robes, the genuine sapphire hung prominently around her neck, casting an eerie glow.

Leonora, with the chilling elegance that only she could possess, raised her hand for silence. The murmurs of the crowd faded into an apprehensive hush, every eye fixed on the enigmatic matriarch.

"Good people of Venice," her voice, magnified by the silence, echoed throughout the square, "Today marks the dawning of a new era. For too long, our city, a jewel of the seas, has been mired in traditions of the past, shackled by outdated beliefs and held back by the fearful."

She gestured expansively, the gleaming sapphire catching the light with each movement. "Look around you. This city, our beloved Venice, is on the brink of greatness. The waters that surround us are not barriers but pathways to a brighter future."

She paused, letting her words sink in, the force behind the heirloom accentuating her every sentence with an otherworldly gravity. "With my power," she said, touching the sapphire lightly, "and my leadership, we will forge a new destiny for Venice. No longer will we be traders and merchants, subservient to the whims of distant lands. We will rise as rulers, and the world will bow before the might of Venice."

Murmurs of both awe and fear ran through the crowd. Some were entranced by Leonora's vision, while others sensed the dark ambition lurking beneath her words.

"But to achieve this new era, we must first cleans our city of its old ways. Those who stand in the way of progress, whose who cling to outdated beliefs, will be left behind, forgotten to history." Leonora's voice grew colder, her gaze even steelier, challenging anyone to defy her.

"Venice needs unity, but not with the weak and the resistant. We will rid ourselves of those who slow our march towards dominance. To any who dare challenge this vision, who dare undermine our great city's rise, know this: Your defiance will be met with swift and absolute retribution."

Her eyes, enhanced by the eerie glow of the sapphire, swept over the gathered masses. "Every alley, every shadow, every corner of this city will be purged of dissent. The canals will run deep, but not with water - with the consequences of opposition. There will be no hiding. There will be no mercy."

A heavy silence hung over the square, the weight of Leonora's threats pressing down on every soul present. The chilling promise of a Venice where opposition was not just discouraged but eradicated sent shivers down the spines of even the most loyal supporters.

Leonora's fingers caressed the gleaming stone at her throat, almost lovingly, the source of her newfound dominance over the city. "This is our destiny. And together, with this power, we will ascend."

It was in this moment of chilling declaration, while the crowd was held captive by Leonora's commanding presence, that Liliana seized her chance. She had been inching closer to her mother's platform. Using a fistful of cascading petals as a distraction, she deftly reached for the sapphire, attempting to replace it with the meticulously crafted replica in her possession. But as her fingers grazed the genuine stone, it reacted violently, sensing the deception. A blinding blue light radiated from it, illuminating the square in an ethereal glow.

The power of the sapphire flared with such an intensity

that Liliana cried out in pain, the skin on her hand searing from the jewel's fury. The stone pulsed, sending shockwaves of raw energy across the square, causing the ground beneath them to tremble. Windows in the surrounding buildings shattered, and ornate lanterns exploded in showers of flame.

Leonora, caught off-guard by the heirloom's sudden eruption, struggled to contain its power, but it was clear that even she was momentarily overpowered.

Panicking, the gathered masses tried to escape the square. The once organised assembly turned into a chaotic stampede, with people pushing shoving, and trampling over one another in their desperate attempt to flee the wrath of the sapphire.

Giovanni, witnessing his sister's agony from a distance, fought his way through the disarray, trying to reach her. But the barrier of frenzied citizens and the cascading energy from the sapphire made the task near impossible.

Above the chaos, atop the platform, Leonora, or rather the entity possessing her, finally reigned in the sapphire's energy, pulling its power back into the stone, though its malevolent glow remained. She locked eyes with the injured Liliana, the motherly facade gone, replaced by pure, unadulterated rage.

Time seemed to slow as the two women stood amidst the disarray, a mother and daughter divided by a force far greater than their own. A thousand memories, both tender and tumultuous, flashed between them. Yet, as the smoke cleared and the tremors subsided, Liliana knew that the mother she once adored was now a captive to the sapphire's malevolence.

Heart pounding in her chest and tears streaming down her face, Liliana summoned a courage she didn't know she possessed. Using her pain and the chaos around her as a cloak, she surged forward. With a swift movement, driven by both desperation and love, she plunged her dagger into Leonora's side.

A gasp, a choked cry, and then an eerie silence fell over the square. Leonora's eyes, which had burned with fury moments before, now reflected a mix of surprise and sadness. She looked down at the wound, then back at her daughter, understanding flashing in her gaze. As she slumped to the ground, he haunting glow of the sapphire faded, its control relinquished with the death of its host.

For a long moment, the square was enveloped in stunned silence. The monstrous heirloom, the catalyst of so much pain and destruction, now lay dormant and harmless around the neck of the fallen matriarch.

****

The vast square, moments ago a cacophony of panic and terror, now stood shrouded in an oppressive silence, save for the distant murmurs and sobs of the horrified spectators. The grand balcony, which had earlier framed a goddess-like figure proclaiming the dawn of a new era, was now stained with the undeniable mark of tragedy.

Liliana, her hand still clutching the now bloodied dagger, slowly sank to her knees beside her fallen mother. Streams of tears carved pathways down her dirt-streaked face. With trembling hands, she gently cradled Leonora's head, a scene eerily reminiscent of a twisted Pieta.

All around them, Venetians watched in stunned horror. Many had come to the square expecting a momentous proclamation, a new beginning perhaps. Instead, they bore witness to a daughter's unthinkable act. Yet, those who had seen the raw, unchecked power of the sapphire understood the necessity of Liliana's actions.

Giovanni, pushing his way through the crowd, finally reached his sister's side. Without a word, he knelt down, wrapping his arms around both Liliana and their deceased mother, forming a heart-wrenching tableau of grief. Around them, members of their rebellion, faces streaked with tears and ash, began to form a protective circle.

It was a grim reminder that even in victory, there can be profound loss. The malevolence of the sapphire, while quelled, had exacted a heavy price. Liliana's act, though necessary, would forever leave a scar on her soul. And Venice, though saved from imminent destruction, would bear the wounds of this day for generations to come.

****

The city of Venice, with its shimmering canals and grandiose palaces, had always been resilient. But the events that unfolded, driven by the malevolent sapphire, had tested its very foundations. As the waters returned to their gentle ebb and flow, and as the ruins of once majestic buildings were slowly restored, Venice began to heal, but it would never be quite the same.

The days following the tragedy were marked by the

bustling sounds of repair and restoration. The city's residents, while in shock, were resilient. Each cracked stone and damaged archway was painstakingly repaired. But some damages, those not seen by the naked eye, were harder to mend.

The sapphire, the source of so much pain, was carefully placed in an orange box, its lid bearing the crest of the Morosini family. The decision to lock it away was unanimous. It was taken to an undisclosed location, sealed deep within the city's catacombs, with strict instructions that its location should remain a secret, passed down to only a select few through the generations. Its dark allure had cost Venice dearly, and no one wanted to risk its malevolence resurfacing.

Giovanni, after ensuring the safety of the stone, departed from Venice. The memories, the loss of Matteo, the forced hand against his mother, it was all too much for him to bear within the city's walls. He found solace in a tranquil hut, nestled on the outskirts of a serene village, far away from the haunting canals of Venice, just like he and Matteo had dreamed of, a place where that could just be. There, surrounded by nature and distant from the painful reminders, he sought peace. He'd often sit by the window, Matteo's scarf wrapped around him, gazing out into the endless horizon, finding a bittersweet comfort in solitude.

Liliana, with the weight of her lineage on her shoulders, took a different path. She frequented her mother's grave, whispering apologies and prayers, seeking forgiveness not just from Leonora, but from herself. With each visit, she'd place fresh roses by the gravestones, their vibrant reds a stark contrast against the somber grey. Her hands would often find their way to her belly, feeling the faint flutters of new life within. It was a painful reminder of her tryst with Antonio and his untimely demise.

But with time, as her belly grew, so did her resolve. She made it her mission to rebuild the Morosini name, not just for herself, but for the unborn child who would carry forth their legacy. Liliana would ensure that the child would grow up knowing the stories, both the highs and the lows, and would be instilled with the values of love, resilience, and sacrifice.

Thus, Venice, like the tides it was built upon, ebbed and flowed through its moments of sorry and joy. The sun set on a city that had witnessed great tragedy, but with the promise of a brighter dawn on the horizon.

As the months turned to years, the cataclysmic events that had once shaken Venice to its very core slowly receded into the tapestry of its rich history. The structures and streets that bore the brunt of the heirloom's wrath were rebuilt, restored to their former glory. But while the physical scars faded, the emotional wounds, much like the shadowed alleyways of the city, held deeper, more hidden stories.

Whispers of the Morosini legacy traveled through the winding canals, from grand ballrooms to humble taverns. Tales of their courage, the heart-wrenching choices they faced, and the malevolent sapphire that nearly brought Venice to ruin, became the stuff of legends. It served as both a cautionary tale and a testament to the indomitable spirit of the Venetians.

The passage of time enveloped Venice in layers of stories,

mysteries, and renewal. As its tales turned into legends, the weight of past events slowly settled, allowing the City of Canals to breathe and flourish once more.

THE END

Epilogue

The cobblestone streets of London were filled with stories of revolution, royal struggles, and the burgeoning whispers of war. Nestled amongst the various establishments was a quaint and rather curious shop, adorned with the nameplate "Morosini's Mystical Memorabilia."

The shop, brimming with antiques and oddities from all corners of the world, was the proud possession of an elderly gentleman. The name "Morosini" held tales of grandeur from Renaissance Venice, but to the current owner, these were simply tales, old stories meant to allure customers with their charm. He had heard countless tales from his forefathers about a powerful sapphire that had once nearly caused the downfall of Venice, but like many, he dismissed these as fairytales, mere bedtime stories meant for children.

On one cold evening, as the fog enveloped the city, the elderly shopkeeper was locking up for the night. Turning the key in the old, heavy door, he paused to take a final look at this shop from the outside. And for the briefest of moments, he thought he saw something unusual - a soft, fleeting, crimson glow from one of the cabinets inside.

He blinked, attributing the vision to the weariness in his old eyes or perhaps the trickery of the dim streetlights. Shaking his head, he muttered to himself about the perils of age and imagination running wild. Resigned to the belief that his long day had simply taken its toll, he hobbled off down the misty streets to his flat nearby.

But as the fog depend and the streets emptied, Morosini's shop stood silently, guarding its many secrets. Among them, a ruby pendant - inconspicuous in appearance, yet holding within it a dormant power, patiently waiting for the right moment to awaken.

www.ingramcontent.com/pod-product-compliance
Lightning Source LLC
Chambersburg PA
CBHW020610310726
48979CB00008B/1412/J
* 9 7 9 8 2 1 8 2 7 2 6 7 8 *